LEVKASEON

GEN-HEIRS: THE GUARDIANS OF SZIVERIA

SARAH WESTILL

LEVKASEON

Gen-Heirs: The Guardians of Sziveria – A Prequel

Copyright 2021 by Sarah Westill

ISBN 978-1-955293-05-1

Cover Design by For the Muse Designs

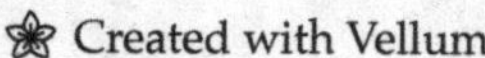 Created with Vellum

Praises for the Gen-Heirs novels –

"[Ms. Westill] has a way of letting you see right into the character's soul, hurt, love, and all."

Baroness Book Trove

"The world Westill created is a fascinating mix of old, new, and futuristic… The world, characters, and plot are complex, immersive, and fascinating, and the non-stop action makes for an exciting read."

One Book More Reviews

"Once again, there is a great mix of steamy romance and intrigue, paving the way for the story to unfold and draw you into it. The characters are fully dimensional, with their quirks and foibles."

The Archaeolibrarian

"Every aspect of the book is very well written; from the good to the bad. Ms. Westill is very skillful in bringing emotions to life and in making her lines smooth, easy, and enjoyable."

Reedsy Reviews

"The suspense, espionage, and intensity of the story kept me from putting this 5-star fantasy story down."

Readers' Favorite

"As steamy as a scalding hot shower, Sarah Westill's words smolder on the page... A heady blend of romance and fantasy... with a dangerous plot and keeps you wanting more!"

Indies Today

OTHER TITLES BY SARAH WESTILL

Levkaseon – A Prequel

Wintersfall

Raiventon

Kynhaven (Jan. 6th 2022)

Asherwick (June 2022)

Ericksen - A Wintervail Special (Nov. 2022)

For world maps and to stay up-to-date on the latest information, be sure to visit www.sarahwestill.com

Dedication and Acknowledgement

For every marriage that needs a second chance…

CONTENT WARNING:
This book contains mature content, including but not
limited to –
Consensual sex (non-graphic)
Action violence

Reader discretion is advised.

WELCOME TO THE GEN-HEIRS WORLD

In the distant future, a major cataclysmic event not only reshaped the world as humanity knew it, but left entire lands uninhabitable. As generations of survivors struggled to endure a fight for territory and resources, humanity regressed into what became known as The Primal Years. A dark and dangerous time that lasted for centuries.

Slowly, civilizations formed in the new nations. Limited means of transportation and communication began to develop in a resource-poor world. Powerful countries arose known as Sziveria, Ruthenia, Italyssa, Westica, and Cairo. New cultures, with their own standards of honor, became global powerhouses.

By 830 Post-Cataclysmic Event (PCE), strong talents are now inherited traits, passed down through genetics. The recipients of an unavoidable hereditary legacy are known as Gen-Heirs. Trains, ships, carriages and if one can afford them, small magnetically powered vehicles move people. Radios are the only means of quick communication besides handwritten messages. Heated water is a luxury. Extreme drops in temperature and harsh arctic winds have forced most food growth indoors, in greenhouses. A dangerously lethal virus known as Human Rabies Syndrome (HRS) plagues the globe. The inhabited world is growing at a slow rate, each unique country striving to exist in harsher, cold climates, and those who survive have become ruthless in their quest to thrive in this new, forsaken world...

THE RANKING SYSTEM:

Guardians of Sziveria

Queen/King Elect
   Prince/Princess Elect
   Arch Guardian
   Prince/Princess
   Shield Guardian
   Master Guardian
   Primary Guardian
   Key Guardian
   Guardian (anyone who serves the realm)

Other Key Terms –

First Intelligence Office (FIO)
   Sziverian National Investigative Division (SNID)
   Haven City Enforcement Services (HCES)
   Medical Science Officer (MSO)
   Medical Science Investigator (MSI)
   Uninhabited Zones (UZ)
   Human Rabies Syndrome (HRS)

1

HUMAN RABIES SYNDROME CONTAINMENT FACILITY
   Haven City, Sziveria
   May 2nd, 832 P.C.E. (Post-Cataclysm Earth)

CIARRA JONATIS, SHIELD GUARDIANESS LEVKASEON, stared at the pacing woman on the other side of the observation glass, and tried to ignore the anxiety burning in her stomach. Clean, well-cared for, her long blonde hair pulled back into a braid, the female patient was the image of perfect health. "How long has she been here again?"

"Sixteen days, Shield Guardianess," the female orderly replied, consulting her clipboard. She pointed down the hall with her pen. A small brass plate pinned to her navy uniform, with the name *Dorie Seever* gleamed in the lamp-lit corridor. "And the patient in observation six-oh-three has been here nineteen days. The patient in six-nineteen has been here thirteen days. All the same. No symptoms."

While the patient in six-nineteen still had a day to go before likely being cleared, the Human Rabies Syndrome virus he was being quarantined for should have already made itself known in the form of an apparent cold. Within a week or two of the symptoms, the virus would go into its active stage and send the patient into contagion mode, seeking any viable host to bite and more aggressively pass on the virus. Prior to active stage, the only way to pass on the viral infection was through sex, where the virus eventually traveled to the spinal cord and slowly up to the brain. It then behaved like the once common, and much feared, animal virus from which HRS received its name.

All three of the patients were partners of confirmed HRS victims. While rare for a partner to remain uninfected, it certainly wasn't impossible. However, three? No, Ciarra had never seen those odds before. What was going on?

"May I see the data, please?" she asked, holding her hand out for the clipboard. She looked each file over, slowly walking down the hall to the next observation room. "Were we able to reach anyone at the Port Anchor containment facility to send us their MedPath?"

Dorie shook her head. "Not yet."

Ciarra sighed and let the papers settle into place. Without a Gen-Heir MedPath – a Medical Empathic Pathologist – they had no true way to rule out the viral infection. The rare touched-based genetically inherited talent only existed in three people in the entirety of Sziveria. With physical contact alone, they could determine any contagion within a patient. One resided in Port Anchor, the other served all the prisons in the Northern Boundary, and the third... Ciarra clenched her jaw. She didn't want to think about the third.

"We can't hold any of them indefinitely." She stopped in front of six-nineteen and looked at a small man curled up on a twin mattress. He'd thrown all the bedding onto the floor. "Let six-oh-three and five-forty-eight go. I want to keep this one another couple days, just to be sure."

Dorie nodded and made notations on the clipboard.

"Is there anything else?" Ciarra asked.

"No, all the other admitted cases have gone as anticipated. These three have been the only anomalies."

In other words, the containment facility had done its job. The quarantined individuals had become active HRS situations. Ciarra shoved her hands deep into her medical coat pockets, her gaze still on the forlorn patient. "Keep me informed if any others occur. And please send me an analysis of the last month."

Hours later, sitting behind her desk at Health Services in the middle of the city, Ciarra's heart plummeted into her stomach. She laid down the information Dorie had sent from the containment facility. When an active HRS case occurred, the victim's most recent partner, or in rarer instances, spouse, was located. They were notified of the situation, questioned, and because most panicked at the mere thought of being exposed to the virus and lied on survival instinct, denial kicking in hard, they were almost always forced into quarantine since they wouldn't go willingly. If after two weeks they showed no symptoms, they could leave. The only time this happened was when a partner had been telling the truth about not having had recent sex with the deceased, and exposure never occurred. Most other instances, an active case occurred in the safety of the containment facility, away from the population.

What Ciarra looked at now was impossible. A small outbreak of HRS had happened over the last few weeks. Not so strange, as when one transpired it usually had a domino effect. Lovers who weren't exclusive always took a chance. If an individual had multiple partners over a week or two, they could expose any number to the virus. Those in turn exposed *their* lovers. The spiral kept widening until fear latched on again in the populace and numbers dwindled. Then the risk-takers would get comfortable again and the pattern would repeat.

According to the documents she read over, the partners or spouses of twenty-four of the thirty-eight cases this month did not become active cases themselves. All but three of them had stated sexual relations within days, or in one case, less than twenty-four hours after the HRS victim went active. The victims had been contagious. Yet, their partners hadn't contracted. That was impossible.

Ciarra sat back in her seat and rubbed her forehead, pain blossoming in her temples. She needed to tell someone. She needed the confirmation only a MedPath could provide. Maybe they weren't *really* seeing HRS, maybe it was some odd side-effect of the recent drug to have popped up in her city known as magic lily dust. The drug was so new they weren't sure what to expect yet.

If Port Anchor were experiencing a similar situation, they wouldn't part with their MedPath. Which might explain their silence on the request. Ciarra could beg the Northern Boundary to part with theirs, but then that would deny three major prisons a crucial medical component. That left one. One who wouldn't speak to her, let alone agree to work with her. Not that she wanted to see him either.

Sighing, Ciarra knew her personal life could not interfere with her Guardian position. Crossing the room to the radio, she input the number for the FIO, knowing if someone could convince her ex-husband to help, it would be the only one who'd stood by his side all those years ago.

"First Intelligence Office, how may I direct your transmission?"

Ciarra took a deep breath. "Guardian Ryan Voklane, please."

Ashen Shores Correctional Facility
May 5th, 832 P.C.E

Terran Kaine paused in hammering a nail into the wooden shelves he and a line of other convicts built. Someone called his felon stamp number again. He considered ignoring the summons. In the five years he'd been incarcerated, no one had bothered to visit. His parents were both dead. They'd left him without siblings. And his wife... Terran finished pounding the pieces of wood together. Thoughts of her were best left alone.

"SZ2051119!" the guard shouted again, walking down the line this time.

Terran sighed and held up his hand, the tattooed alphanumerical code between his left thumb and index finger visible. "Here."

The guard snagged Terran's wrist, comparing the information. "All right, follow me."

Work resumed. The harsh echo of hammer to steel and wood ricocheted off the cement walls, competing with the drone of a saw. Fresh cut pine, cedar and cypress scented the air. Terran waved particulate from in front of his face and couldn't hold in a sneeze. Never failed, the wood dust irritated his nose. Large open bay doors let in ocean air and spring light. Two simple pedal-powered mills worked to cut slabs for the shelving units being assembled. Tomorrow was his turn to drive one of them.

Fatigue settled heavy on his shoulders. Five years into a fifteen-year sentence, seeing beyond tomorrow wasn't something he contemplated often. The guard's keychain rattled with each step. Their bootsteps the only other noise in the narrow, cell-lined corridor. Most guards treated the inmates with an annoyed sense of duty. Or indifference. Terran had learned from prisoner transfers to be thankful for their lack of attention. Other facilities weren't so lucky. He grunted at his sentiment. Yeah, lucky. That was him.

They made several turns before Terran realized they were heading to the visitation rooms. He almost stopped and made demands of the guard. Instead, he took a calming breath and kept the required distance behind the other man. Soon enough he'd know who'd bothered to finally come see him.

The pale blond man with an almost unnatural shade of even paler blue eyes, made Terran's steps falter. Ryan Voklane straightened from the wall he'd been leaning against. The brown, ivy cap perched atop his head matched the pants he wore. A cream shirt and pale brown jacket did nothing to hide the muscular frame of a man who claimed to sit behind a desk all day. The luxurious blend of silk, cotton and wool of Ryan's clothing brought attention to the scratchy hemp weave of Terran's muted gray uniform. He resisted scratching at his chest. Voklane gave a nearly unperceivable nod to the guard, who closed the door without a word.

Terran glanced over his shoulder at the door. "Have some pull with the staff, do you?"

"I have pull with anyone I need to," Voklane replied. He motioned to a chair in front of a narrow, scarred table. "Sit."

Terran eyed the chair and hoped longing didn't show on his face. He hadn't rested in seven hours. "I'm fine. Thanks. What do you want?"

A long-suffering sigh left the Guardian. Ryan yanked out a chair and sat. When Terran still didn't move, he opened his hands in a sign of peace. "Kaine, come on. Sit. We both know you need the break, stop trying to be a scab."

"Am I going to like your reason for being here?" Terran asked.

"You might."

Terran studied the unreadable mask of Voklane's face. A face that looked no older than thirty. He pulled out the chair, the legs scraping on the cement floor, and plopped down. "Five years."

Ryan had the decency to glance away. "I know."

"Five. Years."

Lightning flashed in Ryan's eyes when he looked back. "*I know.* And if I could have changed that, I would have."

Terran settled back, stretching his legs out. "Long

trip out here from Haven City. I understand. But you don't radio, you don't write…"

Voklane dropped his face into his hands on a groan. "I forgot what a smart-ass you can be."

Terran waved a hand in sympathy. "If you'd have bothered to remember I existed, you wouldn't be plagued with this unfortunate memory. What do you want, Guardian Voklane?"

"Ciarra Jonatis reached out to me."

Hurt and anger coalesced into something ugly. Every muscle in Terran tensed. His teeth clenched so hard he was shocked they didn't fragment to dust in his mouth. The chair crashed over as he launched himself upward. "I'm done with this meeting."

"Sit. Down."

Voklane's words held no argument and Terran found himself obeying, sitting after righting the chair, fists clenched.

"Good," Ryan said with a nod. "Now, listen. I know things aren't exactly civil between the two of you—"

"She betrayed me."

A frown bracketed Ryan's mouth. "She didn't betray you. She just… sided with her father."

"Same thing."

"Listen," Ryan ground out again. "Ciarra knew if she showed up, you'd refuse to see her—"

"Yep. Would have fought the guard to make sure I returned to work duty." Terran glanced over his shoulder again. "Considering it now, actually."

Ryan closed his eyes and took a deep breath. "I was going to ease you into this, but you never have done things the easy way. I think he's done it, Terran. I don't know how, but I believe Byron Jonatis figured it out. He's somehow managed to weaponize HRS."

The anger slid away and Terran straightened, pulling closer to the table. "What? When?"

Ryan shook his head. "I don't know. Ciarra only has data going back a month, so at least that long. She doesn't suspect anything more than the anomaly that she's concerned about."

Terran frowned. "Why would a Medical Science Investigator be involved in all that?"

"Besides processing the deceased HRS victims?" Ryan asked with a quirked brow. Then he glanced away again and Terran *knew* he wouldn't like what came next. "She inherited her father's rank. The endowment was approved three years ago."

"She's the new Shield Guardian Levkaseon?"

Ryan nodded. "Guardianess Levkaseon."

A punch to the gut would have hurt less, Terran surmised. "Of course she is."

"She's filled her role well, serving over Haven City Health Services."

Terran flexed his jaw and knocked on the table. "I bet. Her talent is well suited to the rank. She is her father's genetic heir."

"Sometimes being a Gen-Heir isn't enough. She still had to prove herself before the council."

Terran snorted. "Yeah, I'm sure she had to convince them *real* hard."

Ryan proved to be the more mature of the two of them, again, ignoring Terran's sarcasm. "She reached out to me because twenty-four out of thirty-eight confirmed HRS victims have yielded negative physical partner exposure."

Terran blinked. "You mean they didn't contract the virus, despite being sexually active with the victim?"

"Correct."

"That's... impossible."

"Ciarra thought so too. She said you're the only one who could figure this out. I agree."

Terran held his hands out. "From here?"

Ryan reached into his jacket pocket and pulled out a folded piece of paper. "Full pardon, from Arch Guardian Synintel."

Freedom. The opportunity to do what he was born to do once again. The prison had learned quickly the advantages to having a MedPath around, but being asked to randomly go to the medical hall to diagnose didn't compare to working in his lab, dealing with patients, having the respect his touch-based talent once awarded. Ryan Voklane held the chance to return to some semblance of that life between the tips of his fingers. Somehow, Terran remained still. Somehow, he didn't lean across the table and snatch the paper.

"I need more information. Why do you suspect Byron Jonatis?" Terran asked, bracing his arms and leaning forward.

"We don't see HRS situations spring up like this. Usually there is a rush of them, then a lull, then the process repeats. There have been consistent cases, paired with the lack of active partners. Too odd." Ryan shook his head. "I don't like it."

Terran took a deep breath. "Is any of my research left?"

Regret flickered over Voklane's face. "I couldn't get to it in time, I'm sorry."

The news came as no surprise. Terran rapped his

knuckles on the table in thought. "I'd have to start over. And Jonatis will know I'm out, he won't let me get far."

"Ciarra runs things now."

Terran rolled his eyes. "And he owns his daughter."

"I don't know," Ryan said softly, rubbing at his jaw.

Terran leaned further over the small table, his gaze fixed on the Guardian. "She bought his lies five years ago, why would anything have changed? She'll buy them again." Sighing, he looked at the gray cement walls. "I don't see how I'll be able to help you."

"You won't even try?"

Fury resurfaced, burning a path through his chest. "What am I supposed to do, Voklane? Jonatis is so deeply connected, any attempts I make at discovering the truth will be cut off until I end up right back here again. Only I won't return to some nice oceanside facility. I'll be sent to the Northern Boundary, buried in twenty feet of ice, more forgotten than I already am." Terran shook his head. "No. I have ten years. I'll see them through and go somewhere Jonatis and his corruption don't know me."

Ryan flicked the pardon on the table. "You'll have time before he realizes your free."

"You think my ex won't go running to tell her father I'm in Haven City?" Terran snorted. "You're delusional if you believe that."

"I'm not. The Shield Guardianess promised she'd leave her father out of it."

Discomfort twisted in Terran's stomach. He shoved the annoying sensation away. Ciarra didn't deserve, nor want, his compassion. "She won't be able to keep that promise if your suspicions turn out to be true."

"I'm aware of that."

"And she'll distrust any evidence I find, citing my wanting revenge."

"Which, you do," Ryan stated with a shrug.

"Yes, but I won't be like him. Anything I discover will be the truth, not a fabrication."

Ryan shifted in his seat, resting both arms on the table. "So don't go at the research looking to ensnare him. Start from the bottom. Make the connections, if any are to be made, the right way. If Jonatis is guilty, the evidence has to be irrefutable."

"It was before."

"I know, but we didn't move fast enough. I won't make the same mistake twice." Ryan flapped the paper again. "Synintel believes in you, or he wouldn't have managed to free you."

Terran's focus followed the flicker of off-white. "And why would Synintel, the Arch Guardian for the First Intelligence Office, get involved?"

Ryan stilled. "You're kidding, right?"

Terran lifted his brows and opened his palm in question. "He didn't get involved five years ago, when maybe *his* attention would have kept me free. So why now?"

"Only I read your research. We both know what happened after it came to my attention." Ryan sighed. "I brought the current situation to Synintel's desk and reminded him about your previous investigation and Shield Guardianess Levkaseon's request to work with you."

And wasn't that the other problem? If he accepted the pardon and agreed to take on the human rabies syndrome mystery, he'd have no choice but to work with his ex-wife. As the leader over the entirety of

Haven City's health and wellbeing, not working with her would be an impossibility.

Terran wanted to throw the chair he sat in against the wall in a tantrum befitting a toddler. He splayed his hands on the scarred wood and pulled forth a calm he'd had to learn real quick in prison. Hot tempers led to being transferred to a new facility. The Ashen Shores Master Guardian didn't tolerate anything but a peaceful setting. Since Terran enjoyed beaches and a less-than-awful incarceration, he behaved himself.

"Well?" Voklane prompted when Terran remained silent.

"I don't want to come back here," Terran said quietly. "I won't. He'll have to kill me this time."

"I won't let that happen. I'll get you out of the country myself if I have to. Hopefully, we won't have to worry, though."

Terran quirked a smile. "Ever the optimist."

"Someone needs to be." Ryan held the folded paper out. "So, freedom, or remain a prisoner?"

2

CIARRA TURNED ONE DIRECTION, THEN ANOTHER, LOOKING at her reflection in the floor-to-ceiling wardrobe mirror. Most days her golden blonde hair was pulled into a simple bun, kept free from getting tangled or into anything hair should not get into. Her usual uniform of moveable cotton and silk blend pants, a button up shirt and a white lab coat kept her functional and on-par with the rest of the city's health services staff. Today however, was not a work day.

Today she'd see her ex-husband after five years.

Today she'd discover how much he hated her.

Ciarra's shoulders slumped. No matter what she wore, nothing would change. The long, blue pinstripe skirt and elegantly flowing white tunic shirt wouldn't impress him. The glossy fall of her shoulder-length hair wouldn't entice. Or take away the anger he justifiably held toward her. When her father had put in the request for their contract termination, she never thought she'd see him again. The pain of filing had been somewhat dampened by knowing she'd never have to acknowledge the loss beyond being single. She didn't know if she would be strong enough to stand in his presence and not fall apart.

Taking a deep breath, she turned from the mirror. She was a Shield Guardianess now, she didn't have time, or room, for weak emotions. Responsibility meant she'd be an adult when she stepped into Terran's new home. Terran Kaine. The piercing ache in her chest at his surname still took her by surprise. Once, they'd shared the Jonatis name, and he'd given up his own ranking to join in her Shield Guardian position someday. But when the someday had arrived, she'd been alone. She swallowed a lump in her throat.

Poppy, her Stylist Elite, sashayed back into the room. Her round hips made the flowing skirt of orange silk dance around her ankles. "I found it!" she proclaimed, raising a small glass container between her fingers. "I knew I had a sweet shade of pink tint for your cheeks stashed away somewhere."

Make-up wasn't something Ciarra indulged in much. Working long hours, often around dead people who wouldn't care about such things, meant the woman responsible for making Ciarra look beautiful to the world didn't get to do her job often. When Poppy learned Ciarra would be going to a private meeting instead of Health Services, she'd moved too quickly for Ciarra to say no to being primped and preened. A faint dusting of silvery shadow brought out the cloudy-gray color of Ciarra's irises. Using a middle finger, Poppy dabbed on cheek and lip tint until Ciarra took on a healthy, glowing flush.

"Thank you, Poppy. That should be fine," Ciarra said, straightening.

Poppy observed her work and nodded with a smile, her dark green eyes curious. "Yes. Beautiful. I hope this meeting goes as planned. More attempts to secure funding for additional staff at Health Services?"

Ciarra resisted the urge to tie her hair back, to feel more like herself. "No. I'm meeting with an HRS expert."

"Oh." Poppy frowned and tugged at the hem of her purple sweater with big, orange embroidered flowers. "I have been hearing about the unfortunate rise in cases."

"Concerning for Services, to say the least."

"I imagine so. Well, I hope it goes well."

Ciarra muttered her thanks and left the older woman to clean up. Taking a bracing breath, she made her way down the wide spiral staircase to the first floor. She had to get past her father without causing suspicion. She had no intention of going back on her promise to Ryan Voklane.

The stairs opened into a rotunda with a long, angled hall leading to the front and back of the house. Ciarra took a left, where the hall ended into four doorways offset at angles from each other. She entered the first on the left, into the open kitchen and informal dining room. Her father sat at the table, eating his breakfast and going over what appeared to be the menu for the week. While he'd given over the position as Shield Guardian to Health Services, he'd kept a tight hold on everything under his roof. Including her. Ciarra ignored the constriction in her gut. Giving up control was not in her father's nature, no matter how much he tried. If his health had not failed him, she'd still be a MSI under his jurisdiction.

"Good morning, Father," she said, leaning down and giving him a quick kiss on his silver-stubbled cheek.

He grunted and looked her over. "What's with the face paint? You never wear that mess."

"Poppy ambushed me with it this morning," she replied, smiling in gratitude as their home cook placed a plate of warm eggs and fried potatoes in front of her. The delicious scent of pepper and herbs surrounded her. Steaming tea and cold juice followed.

"I thought today was your day off." His watery gray eyes narrowed. "You're dressed to go out."

Ciarra pulled *The Havener* forward, looking over the top headlines. "I had an unexpected meeting come up." She glanced at him. The cotton slate color pants and shirt he wore under a maroon robe hung from his thin frame. Tuffs of uncombed white hair stuck out around his face, haggard and harshly lined in the early morning sun. "Is your Medical Scientist still coming this afternoon?"

"Yes," he said with an eyeroll. "To tell me more bad news, no doubt."

Ciarra tsked and touched her hand to his dry, wrinkled one. "Stop that. They put you on the new herbs. Maybe there's been an improvement."

"You could stop taking extra shifts and start assigning the workload more aggressively like I told you to," he snapped, seeming to ignore they'd been discussing his health, not her choice of how to run Health Services. His face turned an alarming shade of red and he coughed, gasping, papery hacks. When she tried to hand him something to drink, he waved it away. "Stop that. I'm fine. Or I'd be fine if you'd listen for once."

An old argument. Ciarra had learned about a year into her rank, she could do everything Byron Jonatis asked, and he'd still find something to fuss at her about. Nothing would ever be good enough. Nothing would meet his expectation. Too bad the realization had come too late. Now, she was good and stuck in a role she wasn't sure she wanted anymore. Hadn't ever been sure she wanted. But those who worked under Haven City Health Services deserved a competent, compassionate leader, regardless of how the dowager Levkaseon felt about the matter. She took the *Guardianess* part of her rank seriously.

"I do listen to you, Father," she said in appeasement.

"Then someone else would be handling this so-called meeting," he gestured in annoyance, "and you'd be staying home. Where you belong. Taking your day off, like you deserve."

"I won't be long," she said, taking a sip of orange juice to stop a sigh of frustration from escaping.

He shook his head in disgust. "I should be happy your job is more important than my health. And I would be. If you were doing it right. You are in a position of authority, Ciarra. How will anyone take you seriously if you don't start acting your rank?"

Weariness knotted in her chest. "Going to a meeting is not acting below my rank."

"You are an example," he rasped. "Do you want complete chaos? Who cares about schedules? You must hold yourself to the standards you expect of those beneath you."

Ciarra resisted raising a brow. Beneath her? No one

she worked with was ever considered beneath her. Had that been how her father ran Health Services? She hadn't worked under him directly for long enough to have judged his methods. And no one had said much positive, or negative, about her father's tenure. Another abrasive cough shook his entire frame. A female attendant rushed forward with a small cup of thick, golden liquid. Bryon snatched the tincture from the woman and drank it down.

"See what you caused to happen," he said, glaring at Ciarra across the table. "Claim to worry about my health and then trigger a flare-up."

"Fine, I won't go to the meeting," Ciarra lied with ease. Another disturbing skill she'd been learning to hone when it came to him. "I still have some shopping I wanted to get done today, though."

He nodded, his shoulders relaxing. "Good. Shopping is good. Shows we can afford for you to be out, spending and relaxing. And yes, excellent. Poppy made you look pretty enough to be seen. Good plan."

Never mind he'd criticized her appearance not even five minutes ago. Poking around at her breakfast, Ciarra didn't correct him on the *type* of shopping he seemed to think she'd be doing. The ballroom needed new paint and their head housekeeper's son had just welcomed his first grandchild. No way would she interrupt such an important family event over paint. She wanted to pick the colors anyway. The hideous shades of subdued pink paired with muddy brown curtains and trim made the room meant for celebration drab and depressing.

The only benefit she'd noticed, was no one stayed in their home for long. Which seemed to please her father immensely. While he wanted to show off their place in society, he didn't in fact want anyone hanging around. She'd still manage to go to the home décor shop after her meeting with Terran. She had a feeling she'd need the retail time to decompress.

TERRAN FINISHED PLACING THE LAST OF THE VIALS ON A shelf in his new laboratory. Rows of clean glass sparkled in the spacious room with three walls of windows. Facing the south, the room maximized daylight and the natural heat from the bright rays. A perfect space for working. He stepped back and looked everything over. Long tables brimmed with microscopes in different powers, beakers, test tubes in holders, cylinders with valves, the selection rivaled those from his containment facility days. Ryan Voklane had come through and then some. Anything Terran needed for experiments and data discovery would be at his fingertips.

A flash of movement out the windows shifted his focus. He was alone in the sprawling five-thousand square foot house. And he planned to remain that way. Having gone from a six-by-ten-foot cell, the spacious, open floorplan left him feeling oddly exposed. He didn't want anyone else around.

The echo of his boots on marble tile filled the great room on his way through. Quality fabric whispered against his skin with each step, and he found himself having to fist his hands to keep from touching the silk and cashmere blend of his pants and sweater. He'd already caught himself doing so twice today. An improvement from yesterday, where he'd spent almost ten minutes touching each item of clothing in the wardrobe Voklane had left for him before settling on something. At some point, he figured the sense of luxury would wear off. Until then, he had to ignore the ridiculous urge.

Gravel crunched in the drive. Terran opened the front door in time to see a shiny silver Ariot pull to a stop in front of his greenhouse, built at an angle from the house with a breezeway between. The glass structure rose to the same height as the two-story home. Sun glinted off the metal frame and slanted glass roofline.

Shielding his eyes, Terran waited patiently for the driver to exit. Unease knotted his stomach. Only two people knew where he now resided. The magnetic engine, harnessing the power of positive and negative attraction, powered down. The driver's door opened. Burnished-gold hair lifted on the cool, spring breeze. A taller-than-average female frame unfolded from inside. The sun warmed the already golden-beige of her skin.

Terran had anticipated the punch to the gut seeing her would cause. He hadn't expected the flare of desire. Which, looking over curves that had matured in five years, he couldn't fault his body's reaction. She'd always been beautiful. With full high cheeks, almond eyes, and a strong, elegant jawline, she looked every bit the rank she held. Confidence had never been something Ciarra Jonatis lacked.

The wind blew the white tunic blouse against her torso, revealing her perfect breasts, the soft flare of her hips and stomach— molded her skirt to her shapely thighs. Terran breathed out a groan and turned, stalking back into the house. The gravel rasped under her sensible, black monk strap shoes, her steps quick behind him.

"Terran, wait!" she called.

"I see being a Shield Guardianess has treated you well. I didn't know the pay was high enough to afford a personal Ariot," he said, crossing the threshold and leaving the door open for her. "Were the ones assigned from Health Services not good enough for you?"

"Hello to you, too," she breathed, but he noted her steps didn't continue onto the marble.

Stopping, he slowly turned. The bright morning sun backlit her in the doorframe, making the edges of her blonde hair glow. Lemons, and the sweeter, softer scent of freesia flowed around him, carried on the breeze. *Ciarra.* Terran gritted his teeth against the impulse to breathe in deep, to capture the fragrance he could never forget, yet had been denied for too long.

He held his hands at his sides, palms open. "Did you expect some wonderful reunion, Ciarra?"

She glanced away, biting her full bottom lip. "I don't know what I expected."

Terran waited, not sure where to go from here. He had a million questions. Unresolved anger. Bitter hurt. And he was man enough to admit, a broken heart. All from the woman standing a few feet from him.

"The Ariot was a gift from my father when I was approved to take over his Shield Guardian seat," she said softly, nodding toward the vehicle. "He said being able to get around the city without worrying about being assigned a vehicle had been beneficial to him, and he wanted me to have the same."

Terran flexed his jaw. "He could have hired a driver, bought you the best carriage made in Sziveria, and a team of horses to go with for what he paid for that thing."

"I'm aware of that."

Terran narrowed his gaze. "And *I'm* somehow the criminal. Guess you still don't wonder what dear-old-papa is up to, hmm?" He snorted and turned on his heel, heading deeper into the house.

"I don't want to fight about my father." The rapid click of her shoes trailed behind him.

"Yeah. I know."

"Really, Terran. We have more important things to worry about right now than your conspiracies concerning Byron."

Terran bit back his *conspiracies* were the reason he was free. Not her request. "I guess if you're willing to work with a convict, things must have reached a critical point."

"Stop it." Despite the words nearly being whispered, he still heard them.

He halted. Waited. Every muscle tensed.

The fresh, floral scent of her surrounded him as she neared. "Why demean yourself?"

Terran jerked as if she'd slapped him. He rounded on her, knowing by her sudden gasp the rage he could no longer keep in check burned bright. He fisted his left hand and angled it to show off the felon stamp he'd forever carry. "Demean myself? *I am a convict.* Or have you forgotten the fifteen-year sentence I was given for a six-month crime? Because I sure haven't. A crime, I will remind you, I was never guilty of."

"The evidence was there," she said quietly.

Terran found himself being pulled deeper into the old hurt. "I'd been sending excess supplies to the Northern Boundary as aid for over a year, with Jonatis's approval. Then suddenly I'm accused of thievery?"

Terran shook his head. "Some evidence. Guess you still haven't figured out what I'd need with twenty boxes of bandages, four cases of sulfur, and a bottle of powdered ginger root."

"Don't forget the raimarks," she added, but wouldn't meet his gaze.

He snapped his fingers. "Right. The raimarks. Because I had access to the financial accounts to take out the containment facilities funding whenever I felt like it. Forgot about that one."

"The accounts manager—"

He held up a hand to silence her. "I know. Testified I bribed him with a share if he'd make the withdrawal. Only, there weren't any extra raimarks in our account, were there? But I must have hidden them somewhere." He glared. "Trust me. I remember how badly the accusation hearing went against me."

"You may have been convicted of a crime, and served time, but you are still a powerful Gen-Heir," she said evenly, her words slow, convincing. "You are still a necessity to this country. Your talent as a MedPath is important. It's who you are. Not some common criminal, and I refuse to see you as such. So don't ask me to."

3

———

Ciarra knew the heavy thump of her pulse rushing past her ears was visible in her neck, and still she hoped Terran didn't notice. Summer sun, he looked good. Too good. So much more than she remembered. And she remembered a lot. More than she wanted, especially right now.

She'd expected five years to have changed him. They'd sure changed her. Yet the changes to him were… unsettling. While he'd never been weak, or terribly thin, he hadn't been what she'd call a large man. Until now. Broad shoulders, biceps that stretched the fabric of a soft sage green sweater pushed up his forearms, a flat stomach tapered into narrow hips, all pointed to a build she would have no memory of. Prison had made demands of him the lab never had.

Copper highlights tinted his once dark hair a lighter shade of brown. Instead of being neatly cut and combed, the strands fell in a long mass past his shoulders. A leather strap wound around his wrist, accenting once more the defined tendons of a honed body.

Ciarra wanted to touch him with a force that shocked and embarrassed her. She'd once known every intimate secret this man possessed. What he liked. Craved. Demanded. Looking over the masculine angles of his face, her gaze settled on his mouth. Even pressed into a frown, shadowed by a short beard and mustache, the sensual arc of his lips had memories assaulting her. He'd known how to use that sexy mouth in ways that had left her screaming and breathless all at the same time.

His deep set, rich brown eyes narrowed. Ciarra knew if she didn't pull herself together, he'd see right through her. Either one of two things would happen, he'd mock her pathetic state, or remind her how foolish she'd been to throw away what they'd been. What they had. What they could have become.

Swallowing, she quickly looked away and focused on the open, very empty house around her. He hadn't said a word since her little confession. One of many she needed to make. Later. Barren, ice blue walls, a white marble floor, windows void of any coverings made up the home. Or rather, a space he seemed to occupy, nothing more. No greenery. No furniture. Not even a chair or table in the kitchen area to eat at. She figured homes in the Northern Boundary didn't seem so desolate.

"Where is all your furniture?" she asked, her attention moving over empty books shelves, neatly stacked wood near the fireplace, and a single plush chair angled for comfort in front of the heat.

He turned and continued in the direction he'd been going when she'd pissed him off. Something she figured she'd end up doing again. "What furniture?

Recently released from prison, remember? If I had anything, well…"

Right. She'd have it, or the possessions were long gone. She rubbed her chest at an uncomfortable niggle of remorse. "I can send some things over."

"No thanks. It's just me, I'll be fine."

The casually spoken statement stopped her in her tracks. All her life she'd been surrounded by people. Someone cooked, cleaned, laid out her clothes, took care of any aspect of the house that needed care, from the greenhouse to a missing roof tile. She never really considered what that meant until now. Unless she slept, she was never truly *alone*.

Suddenly, the house seemed massive, and much emptier. The echo of his boots pounded through the space. A chill raced along her spine, and she rubbed goosebumps off her arms. Trying to imagine what his life had been like the past five years was an impossible task. She'd never understand. Could never comprehend *wanting* to be reliant only to oneself. Refusing to trust another human under your roof.

A stranger walked away from her. The Terran she'd known no longer lived in his skin. Swallowing a lump of sorrow at the acknowledgement, Ciarra continued following, at a slower pace.

Did you expect some wonderful reunion, Ciarra?

His words whispered back to her, mocking, piercing a heart she'd thought long healed from losing him. She realized now, she *had* in fact expected something. More emotion than anger. Some recognition of what they'd once shared. Naïve and foolish as the hope had been, she'd somehow still clung to the anticipation. They were nothing more than colleagues now, and even that would be an optimistic definition.

Terran crossed a wide threshold into a mostly glass room. Ciarra looked around, impressed. "Wow, so this is where everything is."

He held his arms open. "Most important room in the place. I'm not sure why Voklane put a bed upstairs for me, I'll probably end up just setting up a cot over there."

Ciarra glanced to where he pointed, noting a single walled corner in the entire room. The space wouldn't provide any relief from the rising sun, but would perhaps be warmer than sleeping next to the windows. "A break from the lab is a necessity, you know that. Too much time in here and you risk the research blurring together."

"Can't have that," he muttered, arranging objects on a long, narrow table.

Ciarra missed the pockets of her lab coat, where she'd shove her hands to keep them occupied. She felt... out of place. An unaccustomed situation for her. Since their relationship had been firmly shoved into professional, Ciarra cleared her throat and decided to fall back on what she did best. Work. "Did Guardian Voklane fill you in on what's happening?"

He strode across the spacious room to a desk she hadn't noticed before, positioned to make sure the sun would never blind him no matter when it angled in the sky. "What he could."

"I assume all this is his doing?" she asked with another glance around. She leisurely strolled the room, taking in all the equipment.

Searching through a small stack of files, he didn't

bother to look up. "I certainly had no way of acquiring any of it."

Ciarra sighed and slapped her palms against her thighs, once again caught off guard by her lack of control over the situation. "I'll… be right back. I have the files in my Ariot."

He may have grunted in reply, she couldn't be sure since he didn't bother to turn from the desk and she didn't wait around to notice any other response. Ciarra walked through the empty length of his house to the still open front door. Outside, she pulled herself together. To let the brisk wind, chirping birds and fluttering leaves surround and center her.

The worst of the arctic winds had dissipated. By the middle of June, they would be gone until late September, when they'd slowly return from the north, leaving everything frozen in their path. For now, providing one didn't get caught outside after the sun went down, the days were pleasant. Not quite warm, but comfortable.

When the worst of her distress had slid away, Ciarra went to her little vehicle and pulled a box from the passenger seat. Only two riders fit inside an Ariot. There simply weren't resources for anything larger. Bracing the box in her arms, she used her foot to close the door. On a deep breath, she headed back to the house, hoping with each step Terran would indeed help.

PAPERS SETTLING ONE AFTER THE OTHER, AND THE FAINT crackle of wood popping in the fireplace were the only sounds in the house. Ciarra had disappeared somewhere after dropping the box off, apparently having noticed Terran wasn't in the mood for conversation. He didn't know if she remained on the property, or if she'd become fed up enough to leave. Didn't honestly know what outcome he'd prefer. Which left him irritated. Thoughts of her needed to remain categorized. Professional. If they were simply working together, he wouldn't care one way or another where she was, as long as he had a way to reach her when necessary. Personally however... Growling, he resisted the urge to rake his hands through his hair. There could be no *personal*.

Unable to remain focused on the pages of bad news collecting before him, Terran sat back in the desk chair. He rubbed the bridge of his nose and tried to digest the information he'd spent the day reading. He had questions, and only one person had answers. With a groan, he stood. One way or another, he had to find her.

Daylight barely clung in the sky, turning the clouds a spectacular shade of orange, vivid pink, and rich violet. A fire burned in the large living room hearth, causing him to raise a brow. He looked around the open space. The only place to sit was empty. He went upstairs, did a quick search of the four bedrooms, and also found them unoccupied.

A glance out the second story window revealed Ciarra's Ariot still parked where she'd left it this morning. Terran braced a forearm on the window frame above him and stared. She was still somewhere on the property. His heart kicked at the confirmation. A physical reaction he ignored as he straightened. Disregarding the attraction between them was something he needed to do every time he saw her. No matter how much his body protested.

Since the search of the house proved fruitless, the greenhouse was the next option. Exploring the space hadn't been a priority, so he had no idea what he'd be walking into. The abandoned, weed-filled enclosure, with a lone spindly tree made him stop in the entryway. Brick paths had once wound through, but only a few poked free of mud washes, tuffs of wildflowers, and grass clumps. Glancing up he noted several open panes that had allowed the elements, and desperate seeds, inside for who knew how many years. The tenacity of the plant life clinging to existence anywhere roots could manage filled him with grudging respect. He knew how all the determined little plants felt. Despite the odds stacked against them, they'd found a way to survive, and if not thrive, then at least persevere.

"You have some tomatoes," Ciarra said softly from behind and to his right. Terran turned, finding her perched on an old work table, looking completely out of place amongst the dirt and green algae-coated windows. "I think a few zucchinis too, and definitely some peas. I don't think peas ever die." She lifted her chin and waved. "They're spread everywhere in here."

Terran picked his way through the hip high reed grass, the sharp edges scratching across his pants. "And how is it you know about pea plants?"

"Our botanist doubled as my nanny for several years, remember?" The grass swayed and rustled behind as she followed. "At least, I think I told you about that," she mumbled.

"You may have," Terran admitted, pushing larger stalks away, surprised to find the deeper in he went, the thicker the plants became. The path disappeared completely until he forged his own way. At the lone, pitiful tree, he touched the slender trunk and moved up to a thin branch. Though lacking in care, the bark and leaves were healthy. He smiled. "Huh. I have an apple tree, too."

"And you know about an apple tree, how?" she asked as she leaned around, her cloud-gray eyes curious.

He released the branch and walked deeper into the grassy jungle, searching out other treasures. "If you didn't do your time in the greenhouses at Ashen Shores, you didn't eat."

"Sounds fair," she mused, moving from behind to beside him. Seeds and pollen dust covered her silk tunic shirt and dark skirt.

Terran shrugged. "Fair as prison can be, I guess."

"Was it really awful?" The question was whispered, mingling and floating with the sway of grass around them.

Somehow the words managed to separate enough for him to catch. He swallowed a lump of anxiety. Blinked away an angry retort. "Losing freedom is never anything less."

Silence met his reply. What else was there to say? Touching his palms to the rough tips of the grass, Terran redirected his thoughts, took charge of the conversation. "Have there been any more active cases since my pardon?"

She sighed, mimicking his gesture, the flowers caressing her open hands. "Five."

The number stopped him cold. "Five?" he asked in

disbelief, turning to face her. "Are they connected to each other?"

"So far, no, not that I've been able to find. I thought I included the data in the box I handed to you."

Terran thought back to what he'd read over. "I haven't made it to the bottom of the box, so maybe it's in there and I haven't seen it yet."

She frowned. "They would have been on top, since I put them in this morning. I'd only finished writing the rest of my notes last night before I left Health Services."

A sense of old urgency had him turning around. He'd been here before. Five years ago, when he'd come so close to proving the truth, only for everything to crash down around him. Ciarra appeared oblivious. As though the thought of someone stealing her documents never occurred to her. Terran trudged back through the unforgiving depths of waist-high weeds without a backwards glance.

"Terra-aan!" His name died on a shriek of surprise.

Whipping around, muscles bunched and ready, he found... nothing. Birds fluttered and squawked from their perches along the open beams above. The minor breeze allowed to enter from the open door and windows ruffled the seedy tops of the grass.

"Ciarra?" Terran called, easing his way back to where they'd been standing.

A muffled, choking sound preceded the violent rustle of underbrush. Terran picked up the pace. Ciarra pushed herself up from where she'd landed, face first, tangled in what appeared to be a pea vine competing with morning glories. She spit out a mouthful of dead plant matter and dirt. Twigs and leaves poked out of her hair at odd angles. Grime smudged her chin, cheek and coated her hands all the way to her wrists.

Terran squatted down to help her rise into a sitting position, noting a tear in her skirt near her knee, filthy streaks on her shirt, and that one of her shoes had slipped free. She swept her hands down her face and dropped her chin to her chest on a heavy, disgruntled sigh.

"Wow, well, I guess it's a good thing I wasn't trying to make a good impression, isn't it?" She brushed flecks of dirt and crushed leaves from her clothing and hair.

A trickle of blood slid down her knuckle. Terran grasped her hand before he could think twice about the repercussions. Heat sizzled up his arm. The softness of her palm under his rougher fingertips made him want to explore more. To slide his touch along her wrist, wondering if a caress along the sensitive skin on the inside of her forearm still had the power to make her squirm. To cause her breath to hitch.

Not the time. Not the place. Not his woman anymore.

"Does this hurt?" he asked, using his thumb to touch below the injury.

She slid her hand free, but not before he caught the faint tremor in her fingers. "N-no, I'm fine, thanks."

Their touching affected her as well. Interesting. Terran didn't want to think about what that meant. He stood, took a step away, and looked for her missing shoe. The undergrowth offered no clues. "When did you lose your shoe?"

"My what?" Confusion darkened her eyes. She brushed hair from her face, streaking more dirt across her cheeks.

Terran pointed at her bare toes. "Your shoe."

"Oh." She wiggled her naked toes and muttered, "Well, damn." Growling, she rolled onto her knees and pushed herself up. "Never mind my shoe, we'll never figure out where it flew off to until someone takes care of this weed garden."

Terran glanced around. "I like my weed garden. They seem fairly content to live in here. I'm not sure when I'll have the time to do much more than clear a spot for a vegetable bed or two."

She took a step, grimaced, limped forward another few steps before stopping on a curse and inspecting her foot. "Well, it's your greenhouse. But really, I'd imagine with this house, Voklane must be giving you some sort of ranked wage. You can afford to hire a botanist and a gardener."

The notion of strangers having access to his home, to *him*, left him twitchy. Terran shook off the sensation. "I'm sure I could."

Ciarra sighed, tested a new spot with her bare toes. "But you won't."

Terran took two large steps and scooped her into his arms. She squeaked and clung to his shoulders on instinct, gripping him tight to keep from falling. "Don't need glass or thorns in your foot. I have no idea what's underneath any of this, and neither do you."

She didn't argue. In fact, she didn't make another sound. Her hold relaxed on his shoulders, though her body remained stiff and still. Delicate curves and firm muscles pressed into his chest and shifted under his fingers. The clean, floral scent of her mingled with grass and earth. So different from the salty air and stench of sweat after a day of hard labor he'd grown accustomed to. Unable to resist, he breathed in deep, savoring the aroma of freedom. All he'd have to do is turn his head and his mouth would be near enough to hers to kiss. Her throat would be close enough to explore with his tongue.

Once outside, he set her down and then continued walking, afraid if he took even a second, he'd linger. Test her resolve, and his own. Brush his fingers over her smooth skin. Maybe see if she tasted as sweet as remembered. He wanted to. Yearned to see the flash of desire he'd caught earlier when she'd looked him over. Wanted to know if they'd burn as hot as they once had.

A sweep of cool air did little to calm his blood. Terran flexed his hands, forcing himself to center. Damn his body for betraying him. For feeling *anything* for Ciarra Jonatis. Once was enough to have his heart ripped out and held bloody in her hands. A repeat of the experience might very well leave him dead.

"Still keep a change of clothes with you?" he called over his shoulder, reaching for the side door into the house.

"In my Ariot, yes."

"Good." He yanked the door open harder than necessary. "The shower upstairs is heated. Go ahead while I look through the rest of the papers. We can talk when you're cleaned up."

WATER DRIPPED DOWN CIARRA'S BACK AND PUDDLED ON the cold, tile floor beneath her feet. She scrubbed her face dry, trying not to think about where she stood. Naked. While she could have used any of the other three showers in the upstairs part of the house, none of them had soap. The familiar smokey amber scent of his soap had brought too many memories rushing through her mind. She pressed her face into the towel and bit back a scream of frustration.

Coming to his house had been a mistake. At least, coming alone had. She should have made sure Voklane could be present and act as a buffer. Because apparently Ciarra lacked the ability to control her libido around the man. Carried in his arms as though she weighed nothing, with his heat pressed intimately against her, she'd almost slid her fingers into his hair. Somehow managed not to caress his back to find out how each step felt beneath her palms. He'd been achingly familiar, and yet so different.

Ciarra rubbed her body dry and reminded herself she was a professional. A Medical Science Investigator holding a Shield Guardian ranking. She had a duty to protect not only those who worked under her at Health Services, but a city full of civilians who relied on her to keep them healthy. Keep them safe. Terran was the key to both.

Dry, she slipped into familiar clothing, her black slacks, a loose bright blue silk shirt and a cream finely spun wool vest. Usually, she paired the outfit with bracelets and a necklace of some sort, but as her emergency outfit, she didn't have anything extra. Not that Terran would care, she figured with a disgusted look at her reflection. So why did she? Sighing, she braided the length of her hair. The wet strands left a damp spot along her back.

She tried to ignore the wide bed, all the more intimate by the single lamp burning near the door. The intricately carved design drew her attention. Before she realized, she stood at the footboard, her fingers tracing over the unbelievable scene of a warm spring field, complete with bee's flitting from flower to flower. Wood dyes brought small details to life. The bed itself was unmade. Dark blue sheets and a stuffed silvery blue comforter had been kicked aside and left to lie. No one was around to make the bed for him, and he clearly didn't care if the blankets were left unkept.

Ciarra backed away from the bed, away from the temptation of sheets holding his scent. She practically ran down the stairs, her feet slapping on the polished wood. The sun had long set, and she'd made the mistake of hanging around Terran's property instead of accomplishing the fake shopping she'd lied to her father about. Hopefully, the elder Jonatis would be in bed by the time she walked in the door.

Downstairs, the lights were as dim as above, even in the lab. Only two lamps burned there, one in the center of the room, and one at the desk Terran sat hunched over, flipping through papers. Ciarra stopped in the doorway and watched. An ache settled in her chest. Once, this had been a common sight. He'd never learned when to close a file, when to lay the work down and rest. She'd always had to be the one to slip the reports away, to take his hand and walk him to bed.

"Are they there?" she asked, stepping the rest of the way into the room.

"No." The single word somehow still carried the weight of his distraction.

Ciarra frowned and went to the box perched on the desk corner. "How can that be? I set them on top myself when I finished."

"And no one else had access to it?" he asked, bracing his forearms on the desk and meeting her stare.

"No, I was home. I left everything sitting on my desk and carried it to the Ariot this morning when I left." She pulled her bottom lip into her mouth. "Maybe I left them on my desk after all." Sighing, she rubbed the back of her neck in frustration. "I must have. I'm so sorry."

A skeptical frown twisted his face, but he remained silent.

Her hands dropped to her thighs on a loud slap. "Well, what do you think about everything else?"

"I think," he began, attention back to the papers, "that I need to go to the containment facility and see all the current quarantine cases."

"*All* of them?"

A paper crinkled as he flipped to a new sheet. "Yes. I need an idea of what I'm dealing with. Actual people will give me more information than data on them."

"Of course," she sighed, rubbing her palms on her slacks. "I forgot your process."

"Five years will do that," he said dryly.

"It's been difficult without you," she said before she could stop the words.

"I'd imagine not having a MedPath became an adjustment for the city after I was sent away." He dropped the documents he had and relaxed in the chair. "I was honestly surprised they didn't put more effort into making sure I didn't get convicted. Then again, I probably shouldn't be since no one was allowed to come to my defense."

Ciarra drew her brows together and leaned her butt against the edge of the desk. "What do you mean?"

Shrugging, he reached for a pen. "Just that. You weren't even there, and I'd like to think had you been, you would have maybe stood up for me."

Her breath caught and she looked away, knowing the guilt she'd failed to bury for so many years would be clear. "I would have been," she said quietly.

"But?"

Cowardice wasn't a word Ciarra associated with herself. And yet, she swallowed and chose to ignore the question, not ready to face the consequences of the past. "What time in the morning do you want me to be here to pick you up?"

He stared at her, his dark eyes narrowed. Somehow, she didn't fidget under his inspection. "I know how to get to the facility. I'll meet you there."

She caught a sigh of relief at his letting the question go. "The Ariot is faster, and your house is on the way."

The pen flipped between his fingers. His gaze remained locked on her. "Very well. I want to be there before first in-processing begins."

Ciarra's eyes widened. "But that's at dawn."

"Problem?"

She cleared her throat. "No… no problem."

A glimmer twinkled in his eyes but didn't reach his mouth. "Still hate mornings, hmm?"

"No," she said, straightening and looking down at him. "Since becoming a Shield Guardian, I have to get up early every morning, I'm used to it."

"No more night shifts?"

She shook her head. "Only in an emergency."

He caught the pen mid-flip. "You handle after hours issues?"

"I handle all issues it feels like most days."

Terran's brows drew together. "Your father didn't do that."

She pushed away from the desk. "I think you will find, I'm not my father."

His gaze did a slow, lazy sweep down her body. Warmth suffused her cheeks, and she resisted the need to fidget. When his eyes finally met hers again, they were filled with heat. "I should hope not."

4

A DESPERATE SORT OF CALM INFUSED THE GROUNDS OF THE
Haven City HRS Containment Facility. Everyone knew
they were either a dead-person-walking or caring for
one. At least, that had been the case when he'd worked
on the premise. Now, he figured, some had a glimmer
of hope that perhaps they wouldn't get sick when they
were placed into quarantine. And recently a few had
such a fate.

Taking a deep breath, Terran pulled the edges of his
white Medical Scientist coat together. Voklane had left
three hanging in the closet with Terran's name, Gen-
Heir talent, and academic achievements stitched in bold
black letters on the left breast. The simple garment had
gone a long way to bring back his confidence. While
yes, he claimed an impressive genetically inherited gift,
he also had years of medical training. An achievement
he'd been denied while locked away. Even though the
prison had utilized his MedPath ability when necessary,
they hadn't allowed him to practice medicine.

A sense of anticipation and purpose flowed through

him. He took a deep breath and lifted his face to the brightening sky. Behind him the rumble of a carriage bringing in the first potential patient sounded on the brick drive. Ciarra shifted down the wide walkway, leaving room for the staff to greet and begin the processing of the stricken woman helped from the hired carriage. Another attendant handled the fee for the driver. Rides to the facility were a matter of national health and were provided by the country.

Terran kept his hands stuffed in his pockets, watching the exchange. "Not much has changed."

"No reason to fix what isn't broken," Ciarra said quietly.

The small group disappeared inside. Terran signaled to the doors when she made no move to leave from her spot on the sidewalk. "Shall we?"

"Yes, absolutely," she said with a shake of her head. "Sorry."

"Does something have you distracted?"

"Besides this entire situation?" she asked on a chuckle. "I guess... I suppose I'm just trying to get used to seeing Kaine after your name again."

The admission made him stop in disbelief. He stared at her. "Did you really think I'd keep my accuser's name?"

She met his eyes for second before looking beyond him. "It's my name."

"It's your father's," he snarled, anger he couldn't seem to let go once again simmering deep in his stomach. Terran turned away and fisted his hands, trying to gather back control. "It's a name I'll never take again."

Her sharp inhale carried in the quiet of morning. Yes, he knew what his words meant. If she'd held any hope they'd be able to rebuild what they'd lost, he'd destroyed the chance. Anyone she married had to agree to take on the Jonatis name. Six years ago, he'd been more than happy to be involved with the powerful family, to carry on their legacy. Now he knew the level of corruption far outweighed any honor they may have once possessed. Or, Ciarra could leave her Shield Guardian rank. A choice Terran didn't see her making. Not that a future with her was an option. Ever again.

Forcing his thoughts back to the situation at hand, he turned and headed to the front doors. "Do I need you to check in?"

"Only if Guardian Voklane didn't get you credentials," she said, her voice subdued.

Terran patted his coat pockets, then his pants, feeling for the lanyard with a thick, pressed board identification badge. He found it tucked into his back pocket, yanked the cord free and lifted it for her to inspect. FIO issued, he had no doubts it'd pass her examination. "This?"

She grasped the dangling ID and read over the printed info. "Yes, that will suffice. Just show it at the reception counter." The badge swung free from her fingers and she shoved her hands into her own lab coat. "So, you *are* working for First Intelligence."

"Yes." He looped the ID around his neck. "Voklane thought that would be best, all things considered. I agreed. While technically this is more of a Sziverian National Investigation Division problem, the Arch Guardian over intel teams wanted the issue handled by the FIO. I'm just doing what I'm told, the two agencies can fight it out."

She visibly swallowed. The Arch Guardian's of

Sziveria were the most powerful force in the realm, aside from the Queen-Elect. They oversaw specific areas of government. "Arch Guardian Synintel knows about the HRS problem?"

"I think the whole city knows by now, Ciarra. Haven City hasn't had this level of outbreak in..." Terran wracked his memory for the last known major human rabies syndrome epidemic and came up blank. "Well, not in my career. Haven't the papers been writing on the crisis?"

She walked inside as he held the door open. "We at Health Services try to avoid words like *crisis*," she stated between clenched teeth. "And as of this morning, nothing has been reported, no."

Terran stared at her in disbelief. "How? The problem has been happening for over a month. How is no one at *Haven City Chronicle* or, *The Havener*, who loves to print gossip and sensational pieces, *not* talking about this?"

"I don't know, they just aren't," she said in exasperation. "It's not a conspiracy, Terran. No one cares yet, and I'd like to keep things that way."

At the reception desk, he handed over his badge and waited to be signed in as a visitor. He didn't recognize the young man and wondered how much of the staff remained since he'd worked in the building. The administrator insisted on the extra security level, taking Terran's thumb print to compare under a magnifying glass to confirm his identity. Ciarra went behind the desk and collected a clipboard, several chart papers, and a pen. She wrote something on the top sheet and then handed the collection over to Terran.

When the young man handed the badge back, his hazel eyes were wide. "Are you really a MedPath?"

"Yes." Terran slipped the ID around his neck.

The young man moved his hands under the desk, his color fading. A reaction Terran was used to. The fear of learning you may carry a pathogen made everyone nervous around him, even if they had nothing to worry about. The receptionist glanced at Ciarra. "Shield Guardianess Levkaseon, good to see you."

"Tyler," she greeted with a nod. "We'll be coming and going throughout the day."

"You're good to go." Tyler patted the log book and quickly set a brass key onto the counter. "All signed in, no need to stop back here. I'll make sure Cathy knows at shift change."

Terran pocketed the key; the only way in to certain corridors, or out certain doors. They headed down the hallway, clearly marked by running pale blue lines, to processing. While most potential patients were met at the door, some slipped in unnoticed, either intentionally or because the staff was otherwise occupied. Terran pushed open the one-way door and halted. Seven faces turned to stare at him. Five belonging to possible patients.

"Damn it," Ciarra whispered on a gasp. "I have to go make a radio call."

Obviously, someone at Health Services hadn't informed her about another cluster outbreak. Terran waited until the door closed before approaching the chairs and the attendants. He held out his badge and touched underneath his name on his coat.

"I'm Terran Kaine. I'm a Medical Empathic Pathologist sent to help. I can determine with a touch whether or not you belong here." He pointed at a pale blue door to the left. "You'll be brought to me one at a time, in private, into that room. Any questions?"

"In what order?" an older female attendant with a clipboard asked.

"Any you choose," Terran answered, opening the examination room. He waited, his back pressed to the open door while the first chosen entered.

A young woman shuffled in. Her hair fell in a disheveled braid. Her blue-green eyes, red and puffy, looked anywhere but at him. Terran allowed the door to swing closed and went to open the curtains to let light fully into the small room. White painted walls and tile floor allowed the sun to reflect into the space. One chair sat in the middle, where the patient would usually answer a series of questions. With Terran present, there would be no need for questions or sitting.

He cast her a reassuring smile, the best he could do given the circumstance, and held his palm open. "Can I see your arm, please?"

Trembling, she reached out. Her gaze dropped as he wrapped a hand around her wrist, his fingers pressing into the soft underside of her forearm. "Y-you're a former prisoner?"

Terran took a deep breath and closed his eyes. "Yes."

"What did you do?" she asked softly.

Blood cells, rich, oxygenated, healthy, flowed underneath his touch. He took another breath, focusing his inherited ability. "I trusted the wrong man."

"Me too," she whispered on a tearful breath.

Like a high-powered microscope, his touch revealed the hidden life in her veins. Bright and dark red cells rushed by in opposite directions, giving and taking in a rhythm familiar in almost every living creature. He took his time, looking for the tiny microbe that didn't belong. Only healthy blood met his inspection. Not even extra white blood cells were present indicating an immune response to infection. Carefully, he went deeper, threading his way through the veins in her arm to the nearest lymph node, where if any contagion hid inside her, he'd be able to find the evidence.

When that turned up negative, he went even deeper, to her spinal cord, just to be certain. The HRS virus took a slow journey from the infection point to the spine, where it infested the brain and eventually led to a complete takeover and the rabid, zombie-like state of seeking additional hosts to infect. Clear, uncontaminated fluid met his scrutiny. Slowly, he unwrapped his hand and let his mind empty before opening his eyes.

"You're perfectly healthy," he announced. "No infection."

She covered her mouth with shaking hands, tears swelling in her eyes. "H-how is that possible?"

"I'm not sure yet." Terran lifted the clipboard Ciarra had handed him earlier and clicked the pen. He wrote his first set of notes and asked the woman questions. When he was satisfied with her answers, he released her.

He completed the process on the other four waiting to be admitted, and found like the first woman, they were all free of the virus. Still making notes as thoughts occurred to him, he slowly wound through the halls looking for Ciarra on his way to the quarantine wing. A male attendant sat at the station, while another looked over a paper and dishes of prepared food to be distributed. A name tag revealed the man behind the desk was Bruce and meal distribution was Steve.

Bruce acknowledged him first. "Can I help you?"

"Yes, I need to see," he consulted Ciarra's notes, "the patients in six-nineteen, six-eleven, five-sixty-four, and six-thirty-two."

The two men exchanged a look. "See them?"

Terran pointed to the letters on his lab coat. "MedPath."

Steve blinked and released an expletive. "I thought that talent was a myth."

Terran kept a smile internal, none of the reactions he'd had today were new. "Nope."

Bruce looked at Steve again and then back to Terran. "Did they give you a key?"

"Yes, I have one."

Steve motioned forward. "Go ahead, the rooms are marked."

Terran pointed at the food. "Do you mind? Are there any bite victims in containment?"

"Three, but they're on the other floor."

"I can take these patients their meals, then."

"Sure." Bruce nudged the rolling cart to him. "Thanks."

The cart squeaked with each turn of the wobbly wheels. Terran glanced at the room numbers as he walked by, never having figured out the odd jump in sequences. He stopped at five-sixty-four and looked through the thick observation glass to the huddled patient beyond. A bathroom was the only awarded privacy, and even that was minor since there was no door. The staff had to be able to see progress if any was to be observed. When the virus went active, someone would stand and watch the entire awful, desperate process until the victim succumbed and died.

Terran consulted Ciarra's notes. Patient in five-sixty-four had been admitted three days ago. With a tray of food balanced on one hand, and his clipboard tucked under his arm, he unlocked the door.

A SENSE OF INEVITABLE DOOM HUNG OVER CIARRA LIKE A dark, rumbling cloud. She pressed her middle fingers to her temples and rubbed small circles. The process did little to help unravel the muddled mess in her brain, or the forming ache.

"All of them?" she asked, needing the confirmation one more time, even though she knew the information wouldn't have changed from one second to the next.

"Yes, all the potential patients today, and the ones admitted before my pardon," Terran confirmed.

"I have eight confirmed active cases in the Health Services morgue. How is this possible?"

"I'll figure it out," he vowed, tucking the clipboard under his arm. "It's why I was pardoned. I just need more information. Can you take me to the morgue?"

Ciarra didn't like to think the only reason Terran had been released was to solve her problem. But then she'd have to admit he never belonged in prison, that everything leveled against him had been false.

Which would make her father a liar.

Only one of them told the truth. She'd been given Byron's account, but had never had the chance to know Terran's. Now, she was finally learning his side, and doubts were forming. Denied the ability to even speak to him the day of his accusation hearing, and subsequent incarceration, she'd believed what her father had come home and told her. His account full of regret and sympathy for his daughter, Ciarra had trusted his words. And when he'd wrapped her in his arms like he'd done when she was a little girl, she'd clung to the safety and comfort in the storm of her crumbling life. She wanted to weep for the immature young woman she appeared to have been.

She gathered the notes she'd taken from the radio conversation with her assistant and stood. "Yes, we can leave now."

A firm hand grasped her shoulder before she could walk out the room. "Are you okay?" he asked.

"No," she answered honestly. "I'm not."

She pulled away before he questioned further. The hold she had on her nerves was tentative at best. Taking a deep breath, she lifted her chin, putting on the face of a Shield Guardianess in control. Terran dropped off the clipboard, minus the papers, and the key. Ciarra unlocked the door to the outside. Birds chirping and the delicate warmth of the sun greeted her, easing her stress enough to let her release some tension from her muscles. She leaned against the door, keeping it open with her weight while she waited for him.

The Ariot gleamed silver in the mid-afternoon light. Out of place in the middle of nowhere, so far from the city and civilization. A minimum of two hours walking distance from another living person in any direction, the containment facility was truly isolated. In the distance, she could make out the dust of incoming traffic, likely the hired carriages to take back the discharged patients. Such a rarity for the facility, she'd had to make the call to assure whoever took the job they were safe. The word of a Shield Guardian went a long way.

Terran took the door from her. "All the HRS victims are still at Health Services?"

"At least the last five. I can't speak to the three, they may have been sent for cremation already if the orders were put in before I could request them to remain on ice," she answered, crossing the wide drive with him keeping in step beside her.

"Five should be sufficient. All of them would be nice for comparison, but I'm not going to be picky at this point."

The ride back was quiet. Ciarra flexed her hands on the steering column, lost in her own thoughts, trying not to sink into panic the closer they came to the city. She had no clear plan to fix the impending disaster. No idea what even caused the odd cluster of outbreaks. Beside her, Terran looked over his notes, using his thigh to write on when necessary. Traffic and buildings all seemed to appear at once. From fields to civilization, and dirt roads to brick. Ciarra braced for the harsh bump and change in surface. Terran's focus shifted from his research to the urban scenery. He grew still the longer he watched.

"Has it changed much?" Ciarra asked, pulling around a stopped horse and a small cart only to get stuck behind a brave bicyclist.

"Not really," he sighed. "Some fashions, maybe. And there are a lot more Ariots than before."

"Queen-Elect Arnita promised to make sure every ranked Guardian serving the country in a service capacity would have access to their own Ariot if they were within highly populated city limits," Ciarra explained, waiting for pedestrians to cross the street before making a right.

"Service? Like an investigator?"

She nodded. "Yes, or enforcemen, along with any other vital roles within government offices."

"That's a big promise."

"Yes, and the Ariots aren't the best. Some Guardians, who are relied on heavily, will get assigned a better one. Most of the ones I've seen however," she grimaced, "are made of wood with canvas seats. Not comfortable and forget going anywhere outside of late spring and summer. They just aren't warm enough."

His fingers smoothed over the quality fabric of her Ariot's seat and to the polished wood dash. "You would have been given a nicer one, then."

Ciarra fidgeted. "Possibly, yes. I didn't buy this though, as I said yesterday."

"How do you think Byron afforded it?" he asked.

"I don't know his accounts, but I know he's invested well."

Terran made a vague hum, his gaze once again shifting to look outside the vehicle. The five-story gray cement building with Health Services engraved across the front came into view. Ciarra pulled into a small side lot and found a space to park. As with all government buildings, a carriage lane was full of waiting rides or those available for hire. After they exited the Ariot, Ciarra led the way into the building via a side door she unlocked.

The morgue was located in the building's basement. Despite being subterranean, bright lamps blazed, illuminating the off-white walls and pale gray floor. Pine cleanser scented the air, sharp and faintly sweet. Ciarra wiggled her nose, hating the way death still managed to cut through the dense fragrance. They walked the entire length of the corridor to body storage, passing several autopsy rooms with an investigator or two watching in the hall through a wide viewing window. Only the faint echo of their feet made a sound. No one stood guard over the bodies. Where would they go?

Next to the door a file in a holder contained sheets with information on who had been stored in what unit. Ciarra consulted the sheets, walking up to the wall of small metal doors. "Okay," she said on a heavy breath, "the HRS victims are in five-D, one-C, two-C, seven-F, and five-B."

Terran moved to the one closest to him and unsealed the latch. Out of instinctual fear of the contagion contained within, Ciarra took a hasty step back. He yanked the rolling metal bed out and locked it in place. The almost normal body resting on the narrow plank took her by surprise.

"Why does he look different?" she asked before she could stop herself, taking a small step forward.

"I don't know," Terran muttered, his voice distracted.

Ciarra forced herself to take another step closer. The infection would only hurt her if introduced to her blood stream at this point, and the chance of that happening was pretty impossible. "Normally an HRS case, the victim is—"

"Has a gray pallor and is covered in drool and blood," Terran answered, pushing the long sleeve of the victims jacket up. All HRS bodies were left as they were dispatched, as everything was burned. He pointed to a few spots on front of the deceased shirt. "I see some evidence he managed to catch at least one person. No one said anything at the containment facility."

"Bite victims are automatically processed as patients, you know that."

"Are you sure the incident was processed?" He met her stare across the body. "Perhaps that's part of the explanation. Bite victims aren't being caught, or reporting their injuries. Wouldn't be the first time."

Ciarra frowned. "Perhaps."

He took a deep breath, closed his eyes and wrapped his hand around the victim's forearm. Ciarra's pulse kicked. His brows formed a tight V and his jaw clenched.

"What is it?" she asked quietly, her nerves on edge.

"I don't know… something isn't right."

"Is it HRS or something else? Something new?"

"No, it's human rabies syndrome, but…" He shook his head and grumbled. "Something is off with the virus."

"Maybe it's started to decay?"

"Everything has started to decay. Had started before whoever took the gunshot that ended this man's life, you know that." He pulled up the wrinkled, dirty shirt and exposed a pale, abdomen. With his palm open, he pressed his hand onto the body's sunken stomach. "Definitely something."

Not for the first time, Ciarra wondered what it would be like to have a touch-based genetically inherited talent. Unlike hers, a logical talent, that had to be tested and proven before she could fill a Guardian position, or hold a ranked seat. Or in her case, inherit one. Terran's gift could never be questioned. And the value was without equal. Many others claimed a logic-based Gen-Heir status, but only three could claim to be a MedPath. Most touch-based talents were rare, and utilized to their full potential by the Sziverian government.

"What do you see?" she asked.

"The virus, but it's... wrong." He shook his head and removed his hands. "I have to get to my lab."

Sliding the body back into cold storage, he used his hip to close the door and then made the same inspection of the other four bodies. His expression grew grimmer with each quick exam. When the last body slid back into place, he went to the sink and thoroughly decontaminated.

Anxious to know the results, she hovered behind him. "The same?"

"Yes," he said, rinsing a thick layer of soap from his arms. "I'll show you back at my house."

"I can release these?" She laid the file on the counter and reached for a pen.

"Yes, I won't need to see them again."

5

———

Terran sketched yet another angle of the virus. While the shape of the virus was close to what he'd become familiar with, a cylinder, with a conical top and flat bottom, the similarities stopped there. The virus he'd worked with previously was covered in thick spikes and had little hooks on the end. This new version had flowerlike buds at the end of the spikes, and the whole cell seemed larger. Finished with one rendering, he reached for a clean sheet to start another.

Ciarra slid the paper off the desk and looked it over. "This is what the virus looks like?"

He nodded. "The one in your current HRS victims, yes."

She turned the paper one way and then another. "And it's different?"

"You don't remember what the virus looks like from Medical Science Academia?"

Flushing, she shook her head and returned the sketch to the desk. "I know I should, but no."

Terran grabbed another sheet of paper and did a

57

quick sketch of the human rabies syndrome virus, as seen by a MedPath. Ancient medical journals from pre-cataclysm days confirmed the virus's identity of origin when compared to the images taken from high-powered microscopes humanity no longer had access to. A sense of longing and wonder filled him again at the thought of long-lost medical capabilities. At what men and women referred to as *doctors* had once had available at their fingertips. Currently, the inhabited world relied on unique gifts like his that were inconceivable before the world had fractured. An interesting trade, to be sure.

After drawing the virus, he explained the different parts to her and pointed out the changes. She nodded and moved in close, until her hip bumped his shoulder and her seductive, feminine scent surrounded him. When she took hold of the sketch, he let it slip free of his hands and returned to adding the minute details locked in his memory from the morgue to his other rendering. The charcoal pencil trembled faintly in his tight grasp. Touching her would be as simple as reaching over and sliding his hand up the length of her thigh, rediscovering her firm, strong legs. Learn if the little spot inside her thigh just before he reached her center still drove her wild.

She was everything he shouldn't want and desperately needed.

Terran angled his head until her legs came into view. He wondered what she'd do if he gave into the temptation. Would she slap his hand away, or welcome his touch? Squeezing his eyes closed, he forced himself to remember she'd left *him*. A week after his arrival at Ashen Shores, he'd received the official documents saying she'd been released from the ten-year contract to him, under the criminal conviction clause. A process she had to initiate.

"You're sure this isn't some weird mutation? Even though we can't see them like you, we still learned they tend to do that," she said, pulling his other drawing closer.

"Perhaps. I'd have to see a recently infected to know. Are any at containment?" he asked.

"I can find out." She turned and leaned against the desk. "I can't see how there wouldn't be though, not with how many active cases we've had."

"And yet, every lover has been uninfected."

Her arm dropped, the paper fluttering against her thigh. "True."

Somehow, Terran kept from rolling his chair to place himself in front of her. Kept from wedging his way between her legs until she straddled him. Thick coils of desire stirred in his veins. The slender stick of coal popped in half between his fingers. She lifted her gaze, her eyes smokey in the shallow fall of light from the desk lamp. Awareness settled so thick between them he was surprised arcs of energy didn't appear. Her body swayed toward him, as if pulled by an invisible strand. Terran leapt from his seat, sending the chair spinning back.

Gasping, she blinked and arched away, shock and hurt flickering in her eyes. "Um…" She rubbed her hand on her thigh and set the paper on the desk. "It's getting late, I should probably go. Do you have a radio in this place?"

He grasped the back of the chair, using it as a shield to keep from giving into temptation. The niggle of guilt at her wounded look would have to remain. "Not yet, but Voklane promised he'd get me one. Eventually."

"Right. Well, then I guess I'll pick you up around the same time as this morning, if there are any patients on the confirmed quarantine floor."

"I don't mind going alone. You have an entire city to handle."

"A city that is in danger until I figure this out. Until *we* figure this out." She shook her head. "No, I want to go, I want to know what you're finding as you make the discoveries. If there's anything I can do to help, no matter how small, I plan to be available."

Terran wanted to tell her the biggest help would be keeping her distance. That every second he spent around her was torture. A test in patience he feared he'd lose at any moment. A reminder of what he couldn't have. What had been stolen from him. From them. But he didn't. Instead, he nodded in agreement, and watched in silence as she left without another word.

THE FAINT GLOW OF LIGHT FROM THE DOWNSTAIRS windows made Ciarra's fingers flex on the steering column. Her father was still awake. The knowledge made anxiety curl in her chest and twist her stomach. She didn't want to go inside. Didn't want to know why he'd stayed up waiting for her, afraid she already knew the answer.

Terran.

Byron still had deep connections at Health Services. Having only been retired three years, many who worked under Ciarra were more loyal to the dowager

Shield Guardian Levkaseon than they'd ever be to her. As soon as she'd walked in the building with her previous husband, the man Byron had sent to prison, her father had likely received a radio transmission. She should have known, should have been prepared for the possibility. Quickly she was learning he hadn't relinquished much control and would want to be kept informed of anything considered important.

Folding her arms over the dash, she dropped her head and let out a long sigh. She hadn't wanted to leave Terran's. Had been so, *so* close asking him if she could stay. By the way he'd looked at her, the unmistakable darkening of his eyes and tautness of his body, she knew with one kiss she could have had her answer. But then, she'd have manipulated him, and she'd be no better than her father in Terran's eyes.

Ciarra wasn't sure when she realized following in Byron Jonatis's footsteps might not be what she wanted. Once, living up to the former Shield Guardian's expectations had been all she'd hoped to achieve. Now? The near fanatic way in which he made demands of her career concerned her. Something had changed, or perhaps whatever bothered her had always been present, she'd just now noticed.

Notes in hand, Ciarra climbed from her Ariot. Frost glittered on the brick and shimmered on all the leaves. Her breath left her in giant puffs of vapor. Come morning, the sun would burn away the cold, but until then, ice reigned. The heels of her boots echoed in the stillness on her way up the walk. A crack of light appeared at the door, someone waiting to open it for her on the other side. Further proof her father was still awake. No one bothered to stay up for her late nights. Once the dowager retired, so did the staff.

Burying her frustration, she nodded to the footman. "Is my father in his study?"

"The library, Guardianess," he corrected, closing the door. "He wishes to see you."

Dread settled like a stone in her stomach. The library was *her* work space. Ciarra took the angled hall to the back of the house, walking through the quiet breakfast room and into the library. Lamps burned brightly in the room. The flutter of pages being shuffled mixed with the pop and crackle of wood burning in the hearth. Her father's thin frame hunched over her desk, littered with documents and opened folders.

"What are you doing?" She rushed across the room. Every drawer in the desk was opened, emptied. Stacks of files lined the floor and chairs shoved to the side. Her entire career unloaded in unorganized chaos.

"Terran Kaine was seen at Health Services with you today. Why did I not know he'd been released from prison?" Byron flipped quickly through several papers. "How could you keep that from me?"

Ciarra tried to make sense of all her work spread out, trying not to panic at all the important case information mixed together with old files she'd only kept around for reference. How would she undo the mess he made? "He was released by the First Intelligence Office."

"Why?" Byron snarled. "All he's good for is seeing a pathogen we already know exists in a body. What sort of help could he possibly be?"

She bit her tongue to keep back an angry retort.

Nothing about Terran was useless. "You didn't feel that way when you arranged our marriage."

Bryon growled and waved a hand, shifting through another collection. "I didn't know he was thief and a liar then."

"I never did understand how excess supplies sent north were considered stealing."

"I didn't approve them. The supplies weren't his to send," her father stated, his tone bored, distracted. "Besides, you know he stole all those raimarks."

Ciarra moved to the nearest chair and tried to see what files were stacked on the seat. "Never proven, am I correct? There was never an account with his name, and the raimarks were never recovered."

Bryon sputtered and slammed his hands on the desk, making her jump. "Why does any of that matter? Because you saw *him*? Nothing has changed, Ciarra. Wherever the raimarks went, only he knows. He must have finally found someone to bribe, and offered them to someone at the FIO for his release. I'll find out who, don't you worry. Until then, stay away from the man. He's no good and I don't want you around him."

"I'm twenty-seven, and I have a city government office to run. I'm sure this won't be the first time I'm asked to work with someone you don't approve of," she stated calmly, though everything in her seethed. Ciarra knew the truth, because she'd been the one to secure Terran's freedom. Doubts about her father grew. Maybe Terran had been telling the truth all along. "Why are you looking through my files?"

"I wanted to see what else you've been hiding from me," he answered, reaching for a new folder.

"Hiding from you?" she asked in disbelief. If anyone

hid something, he was sitting at her desk. Ciarra managed not to throw the accusation at him. "This is *my* work, my Guardianship. I am responsible for every case you're tearing apart!"

"A Guardianship *I* secured for you!" His gnarled hands pounded on the desk, sending loose papers scattering. "You'd be nothing without me. And here you are, betraying me."

Ciarra rushed forward to collect the papers before they made a bigger mess in the room. "Betraying you? Because I've been asked to work with Terran? We're back to this? I've already explained that."

"What lies has he said about me? Tell me! I want to know why you stood there and questioned me. Questioned my right to look through things in *my* house." Byron demanded, rising on shaky legs, his normally ashen face an alarming shade of red. "What has he been telling you?"

Ah, the real reason for the fit of anger, and if she were honest, paranoia. Ciarra remained outwardly docile, composed. Inside, she wanted to flee back to Terran's and demand he tell her all she'd refused to hear before. "What do you think he'd have to say to me, Father?"

The bluster left him and he sagged back into the seat on a choking cough. Ciarra went to her drink cabinet and poured him some water. He accepted the glass with trembling fingers.

"Nothing," he managed after drinking half the contents. "Absolutely nothing. You know how he lies, though. Don't believe a word he has to say. No one else ever has."

But someone was going to start.

6

———————

"WHAT HAPPENED? HOW DID YOU GET EXPOSED?" TERRAN asked his patient, Garrett, a thin, barely twenty-year-old, red-haired man, too young to be sitting on a bed in the containment facility, dying.

Terran wrapped a blood pressure cuff around Garrett's small bicep. Collecting data on confirmed patients used to be a common occurrence in the facility. Not anymore, he mused, as a group of Medical Scientists stood outside the room and watched in tense awe while Terran interacted with a human they viewed to be a monster-in-waiting. Garrett kept flicking his gaze to them, nervous, ashamed. Terran wished, not for the first time, he had a curtain to block off the interview and examination. But hiding such a dangerous pathogen wasn't allowed.

Terran touched the boy's arm before slipping the stethoscope ear-tips into his ears. "Relax, nothing bad is going to happen." Then he amended, "Not yet."

"You can really tell that?" Garrett asked in surprise.

"Sort of." Terran grasped Garrett's wrist and pulled

his arm straight, holding it against his side. "I can tell where the virus has progressed in your body. It's still in your spine. You have at least another day."

By the time the virus reached the brain, the growth was rapid and the active stage would start within hours. At least, Terran assumed such was the case. He'd never been able to study a patient when they moved from one phase to the next. After taking Garrett's blood pressure, Terran recorded the results in the file and removed the stethoscope, draping it back around his neck.

Tears filled Garrett's green-brown eyes. "I keep trying to get used to knowing when I'm going to… you know… but I can't. I don't," he took a deep breath and reached for a tissue to wipe his running nose, "I don't want to die."

"How were you exposed?" Terran asked again, undoing the cuff.

"A friend took me to a party and someone handed me this pink powdery stuff. They told me to put it under my tongue and I'd have a really great time. So, I did."

Terran frowned. "Pink powder?"

"Yeah. Everything felt… different. Better. When I woke up the next morning, I was in bed with three other people." He swallowed and looked away. "I don't remember much."

Terran hummed. "That's a shame."

"Yeah." The kid smiled sadly. "I wish I could remember if it was at least a good time."

Grabbing a glass thermometer from his kit, Terran held it up and opened his mouth, an old habit to show what he wanted the patient to mimic. Garrett's mouth popped open. Terran took his pulse and then counted his respiration rate while he waited on the temperature reading. He recorded the information.

"Definitely running a fever," Terran noted, writing down the numbers. "Which is normal. How else are you feeling?"

"Sore, and tired. My throat hurts."

Terran nodded and wrote the symptoms down, along with where in the body he'd noted the virus. "Also to be expected. Your nose will probably start running at some point today, and you may begin coughing."

"Will I know?" Garrett asked on a whisper. "When I change? Will I know what I'm doing?"

"No," Terran replied softly, reaching into his bag for a specimen vial and collection needle. "There were four of you, but you're the only one here?"

Garrett glanced away. "I'm the only one left."

Terran recalled the outbreak of three Ciarra had mentioned before the five. They were true HRS incidents, unlike the others he suspected were somehow false. "Ah. They must have been further along."

"Wouldn't they have to be, to have infected me?"

Terran nodded. "Yes, but all three of them? They would have had to have been infected at near the same time as well."

Garrett shrugged. "Probably were. I'd just met the guy that invited me." He took a deep breath and flattened his palms on his thighs. "Had I known, I obviously wouldn't have gone, let alone agreed to try some weird drug."

Terran prepared Garrett's arm for a blood sample. "Little stick."

The young man gasped when the needle penetrated his arm. A sensation most in Sziveria weren't familiar with unless they'd needed a rare injection in their lifetime. Viscous, red blood flowed into the vial. Terran collected the full amount and carefully placed the tube with the needle in a wooden box. He'd dispose of all the contents himself. At one time, he'd all the data he needed. But after his incarceration, Byron Jonatis had seen to the disposal of all Terran's research. Now, he had to start over, and he didn't have the time.

Finished with his collections, Terran looked at the downcast young man and held his hand out. "Thank you for allowing me to speak with you."

Garrett sniffled and accepted his hand on a firm grip. "Thanks for treating me like a person. It's been hard, being in here."

Sympathy knotted in Terran's chest. "I know, and I'm sorry for that. But it's good you're here. Admitting yourself was the right thing to do. You saved a lot of lives."

The young patient nodded, a tear sliding down his cheek. "Yeah, I know."

Terran squeezed his shoulder. He wished he had comforting words to say, but there were none. In a day, maybe up to three, the young man would be taken over by a violent virus. For a couple hours he would turn into a zombie in a last-ditch effort to spread the infection before death claimed him. A different reality didn't exist, nothing else could be said.

Ciarra unlocked the thick glass door for him and held it open. The group of onlookers parted. All except Ciarra, who knew he wasn't contagious. She fell in step beside him to the sink and waited while he decontaminated.

"Do you have everything you need?" she asked once he finished and they headed to the stairs.

"I think so."

"And? The virus?"

Terran sighed. "Normal. He's definitely infected. The virus looks as it should, exactly how I remember."

"I don't understand how this is possible," she said, the echo of their boots hitting the steps bounced around the stairwell. "This isn't like the ancient textbooks, where they could manipulate viruses. We don't have the means to make that happen, so how can an altered version of the disease even exist?"

"I don't know." Terran gripped the smooth, wooden handle of his medical case until pain blossomed along his palm. "I didn't know five years ago. I don't know now."

She froze, her foot halfway to the next step and twisted until she half faced him. "What do you mean you didn't know *five years ago*?"

"Just that."

"You've seen this before," she stated in disbelief. Then she rounded on him and her words tripped together, "What— how— when were you— what did you…"

Hinges squeaked, reverberating along the twisting shaft of stairs and Terran held up his hand. "Not here. Not now. Later."

A sharp inhale whistled between her lips. The urge to argue, to demand, burned in her eyes. Then she nodded and pressed her mouth into a tight line. On a whirl, she turned away from him and continued down the stairs. Terran let out a relieved breath and followed, wondering what had changed that she understood talking where others could hear wouldn't be a good idea.

They took the rest of the stairs in silence. Ciarra waved to those she knew, but didn't stop to carry on conversations. They bypassed the front desk for the side door since Terran didn't have to leave anything behind this time. In the Ariot she turned to him.

"All right, talk," she demanded.

"Back at my house, I will," he stated calmly, situating the case at his feet since the small back space was full of her things.

He thought she'd argue, then on a growl she started the ignition process. Seconds later, she zipped out of the drive. Terran braced his hand on the ceiling to keep from being pitched into the window. The ride back to civilization was made in record time. Terran was surprised her Ariot pulled into his driveway in one piece. She'd taken the dirt roads so fast the little vehicle had bumped and jostled the entire time. She leapt out, shaking the frame with the force of her door closing in her rush. When Terran looked at her through the windshield, an eyebrow raised, she opened her arms and gave him a *what are you waiting for* stare.

He was in no great hurry. The outcome was already promised, he'd been down this particular path before, he had no great wish to return. But if his and Ryan Voklane's suspicions turned out to be true, innocent lives depended on him. Heaving a sigh, Terran exited the Ariot, his case in hand. Ciarra bounced on her feet while she waited for him to unlock the front door. Inside, she rounded on him in expectation.

"I don't want to fight," Terran said softly.

"Why would we fight?" she asked, and then blinked and took a step back. "Oh. You think it involves my father."

He sighed and strode past her, heading to the lab.

"I promise I'll listen," she vowed, hurrying to catch up to him. "I won't argue with you."

Terran set the case on his work table next to the highest-powered microscope Voklane had been able to secure for him. Once upon a time, the technology to see even an atom existed. Now, medical scientists like him had to be thankful for the simple technology they could access with the limited resources available to humankind. That he could magnify anything at all was a gift he valued. Someday, perhaps, they could take the technology their most brilliant minds had managed to secure and apply it toward things in the medical field. But he figured the day was long in coming. They barely managed to lay enough track to run the MagnaRail for travel, or secure what was needed to produce Ariots and water heaters for those able to afford such luxuries.

He perched on a stool and opened the case, withdrawing the box with the blood sample. Clearing his mind and shoving personal feelings aside, he focused on the task of learning what he could while his sample was fresh. He unwound a leather strap from his wrist and used it to tie his hair back. "What do you remember, or know, about the accusations leveled against me five years ago?"

She crossed her arms and frowned, her focus following his movements as he prepared slides. "What do the accusations have to do with the virus?"

Terran met her stare. "Everything."

She grabbed a stool from the table behind and sat. "Okay, I'm listening."

Unsure about her change in attitude, Terran watched her. Only curiosity and a hint of concern registered on her face. What did he have to lose anymore? She couldn't exactly dissolve their relationship if she didn't like what he had to say.

"I'm sure you remember, prior to my conviction, *all* HRS incidents were sent to the containment facility," he began, preparing the microscope for the first slide.

Leaning forward, she braced her arms on the polished pale wood surface. "That's right, for research. Even the bodies of those killed in an attack, or an active case."

Terran nodded, rising. "Correct. As a MedPath, I was in a unique position to collect data and help facilitate important research into understanding HRS. I worked with medical scientists in Westica, Gaula, Ravenna, even the Eastern Isles. I communicated with other MedPaths in Ruthenia, the only other country that can boast having those with my talent. By sharing information, we were better able to understand the virus and its impact on our countries."

He picked up the file with his current notes and carried it back to the work table. "Then, about six years ago, a body came from Haven City that had an unusual strain of the virus. I made notes, asked a few fellow Medical Scientists, and dismissed it as an odd anomaly. But then two more cases happened over the span of a few months. All deceased, without any live specimens for comparison."

"Like today?" she asked curiously.

"Sort of," Terran said, positioning the slide into

place. "The victims were homeless, so if they had lovers, no one could ever find out. Most came from the Old City Ruins, and you know how they don't talk. However, even three weeks after arriving, no active cases were reported. By the fourth incident I began to get suspicious. Only the variant produced single instances, it didn't make sense."

"No bite victims?"

Terran shook his head and looked into the eye piece. "No. Reports in the Ruins from the containment unit said the infected acted sluggish. People were able to get away in time."

Ciarra frowned and tapped a finger on the table. "That's odd. Most active cases, the infected is too fast to evade."

"Right, so it was yet another tip the virus I was seeing wasn't natural, wasn't right. I organized a report and sent it to your father with my concerns. If we had a new variant on our hands, we needed to know. If we had some mad scientist working in a lab somewhere, using unknown technology to fabricate a new version of the virus, we needed to know that, too."

Terran took a deep breath and viewed the round cells on the slide. He increased magnification and studied the revealed detail. "When Jonatis finally bothered to get back with me, it was to tell me I was mistaken and stop wasting my time chasing the impossible."

"But you didn't," she guessed.

He turned the knob another click and adjusted the plate to focus at the new magnification. "No, I didn't. Four more cases came through before Jonatis changed the protocol and all deceased active cases were released for immediate cremation. I had a friend who worked as an MSI and would radio when cases came in and sneak me into the basement to examine the bodies. Two additional variants appeared, and when I questioned my friend, I didn't like the direction of the changes. Still no lovers, all the variants were still coming out of the Ruins, but they were getting faster. Two bite victims, both died from their wounds on location." .

"Why didn't you say anything to me?" she asked quietly.

He looked up from the microscope. "Because I suspected your father was somehow involved."

"And you didn't trust me?"

"I didn't trust him," he clarified. "When your father agreed to our marriage contract, it was with the sole goal of seeing the Jonatis line strengthened. Between your genes and mine, we were almost guaranteed to produce a Gen-Heir who could serve as the next Shield Guardian Levkaseon in the necessary medical capacity. Either as a Medical Scientist like you became, or as a MedPath like me.

"Anything that jeopardized the position was a threat Jonatis wouldn't tolerate. Once he knew I suspected something he saw me as an enemy. Your relationship with your father has always been close, and I knew it wouldn't take much for him to convince you I was a liar. Only..." Terran sighed and wrote a few notes inside the folder. "He went a lot farther than I ever imagined."

"The accusations," she murmured.

Terran paused in his notetaking. The helpless frustration from so many years ago threatened to uncoil within him. Several controlled breaths allowed him to push the old anxiety away. "Yes, they came rather unexpectedly, and faster than I could defend against. Not that I was given the option. As I told you, the charity I supported wasn't allowed to speak at my hearing. No one was."

She glanced away and licked her lips. He tried not to focus on the glossy path the pink tip of her tongue left behind. "And then I abandoned you, too."

A fist tightened around his heart. He didn't know how to take her confession, her recognition of how he must have felt in the midst of his chaos. "Yes, well, if your father persuaded you of my guilt as flawlessly as he convinced the judge at my accusation hearing, I imagine my innocence didn't stand much of a chance."

She stared down at her hands, braiding her fingers together. "I..." She released a harsh exhale. "I wish I could sit here and say he was a different man five years ago, that I've seen changes in him recently. But I'm afraid it was my own ignorance and youth that made me blind to what must have always been, and I'm only now seeing things I always should have."

Terran frowned and moved around the microscope, bracing his forearms on the table. "What happened? What's going on?"

Her chin wobbled and she shrugged, her fingers twisting together. "I don't know for sure, except..." She took another deep breath and met his stare, her eyes bright with unshed tears. "He's dying. And in his fear of dying, he's making mistakes I don't think he would have made in front of me before."

"Such as?" Terran prodded gently when she didn't elaborate.

"He tore my office apart looking for evidence I was

trying to betray him," she whispered. "He knows you're out and I'm afraid he's going to do something rash."

"He's worried you've discovered something about the virus," Terran mused, leaning back, his fingers wrapping around the edge of the table. "But he can't take out his own daughter, not when he's put you in a position of authority. He can't discredit you either, not without costing you the Guardianship."

"So, then what do you think he was doing?" she asked, then answered her own question. "Looking to see what I may have known so he could make it disappear." She gasped in outrage and looked away, her cheeks blooming red. "I didn't lose those files on the newest cases. He must have taken them."

"Feels awful, doesn't it?" he whispered.

Her gray eyes lifted. Flashes of shame, anger and frustration shifted through their stormy depths. She opened her mouth on a sharp breath and Terran stood.

"I said I didn't want to fight, and I meant it," he said, clasping his hands behind his back and standing in front of the massive wall of windows. The house Voklane secured for him sat on the city's edge. A barren field stretched for acres until it ended abruptly at a tree line. "I shouldn't have said that."

Fabric rustled before the click of her boots drew closer behind him. "Speaking the truth doesn't mean you wanted a fight. I wasn't going to argue. Yes, knowing my father possibly wanted to hide evidence, to keep me from doing my job, hurts. I'm questioning a lot of things right now, and I won't lie and say I'm processing everything well. I'm confused and... and scared."

Terran fought against the stirring of sympathy at her words. And failed. Ciarra's entire life had been one giant bubble of protection. Byron Jonatis had kept his daughter hidden from anything that might have harmed her. From relationships to the professional world she walked in. Terran knew Byron hadn't released the reins to Ciarra until he'd made sure everything was perfectly in place for her to step in and succeed. Her carefully cultivated world was crumbling, and all she had to support her was a man she'd cast aside, and one the country viewed a criminal.

He didn't want to feel compassion.

Didn't want to care.

Everything in him stretched and yearned to pull her close, to ease her fears, to take away her pain. Despite his intentions to remain callous and cold where she was concerned, Terran's heart had other plans. Wrapping an arm around her shoulders, he pulled her into his chest and tried to convince himself comforting her didn't mean anything. There were no limitations on human kindness. But when the warm softness of her body pressed against him, familiar and welcoming, Terran struggled to remember why she needed to be kept away. From the depths of his conscious, *mine* whispered though him on a tidal wave of desire.

He hugged her tight, until her thighs, stomach and chest crushed to him. Her hands fisted in the fabric at his back, and she buried her face in his throat. The sensation of her breathing deep, taking in his scent, whispered along the sensitive skin at his neck. If he leaned back a fraction and turned his head to the left, his mouth would align with hers. He'd taste her again.

Experience the passion she never could hide from him. Terran's pulse kicked at the urge.

He squeezed his eyes closed and leaned into the thick glass to support their combined weight. Ciarra shifted, just enough to force his knees apart to settle her weight deeper against him, to drive him wild, and make him groan. Her hold disappeared from around his waist and before Terran could stop her, she slipped her fingers into his bound hair. The soft heat of her mouth pressed to his, tentative, gentle, unsure as to the welcome of her kiss.

But Terran could never deny her.

At the delicate questing pressure of her tongue he opened, accepted the sensual, exploring sweep. Her hands tightened in his hair, pulling him closer while she struggled to mold her frame closer to his. Terran's hands slid from her waist to her butt. He filled his palms with her firm curves and lifted, fitting their hips together intimately, reveling in the pleasure of her female form. Too long he'd gone without her. Too long he'd been denied the very thing he'd craved like breathing. And now she stood, temptation in his hands, and Terran didn't know if he had the strength to stop.

7

———

NEED ROLLED THROUGH CIARRA LIKE A MAGNARAIL train without breaks. She was on a collision course with disaster, and she couldn't bring herself to care. No one started a fire in her blood like Terran. *No one.* And she thought to try with other men after he'd been sent away. The pathetic kisses and greedy fumbling of the men she'd considered courting, or rather that her father had sent her way for consideration, had made her realize the passion she'd shared with her husband had been rare. Special. Just like the man.

Emboldened by his acceptance of her embrace, spurred by the need to just *feel*, Ciarra didn't object when he pulled her tighter, fitting their bodies together so perfectly. Nor did she attempt to take control back when his tongue swept into her mouth, exploring and claiming in equal measures. The softness of his hair teased her hands. She buried them deeper until the leather strap holding the mass back fell and his hair tumbled free, caressing her forearms in a feathery brush.

Breaking the kiss, she leaned back and stared at what she'd revealed. Dark hair framed his face. Sunlight glinted off the lighter strands and made his normally chocolatey brown eyes golden. The midday light cast hard shadows on the rugged planes of his cheeks and jaw, glinted on the dampness of his full lips. Ciarra smoothed his hair behind his ears and returned her mouth to his, nipping, teasing, tasting the aftermath of their earlier kiss. He groaned and captured her tongue between his teeth, drawing their embrace deeper.

Desire flashed like lightning. A sizzle of need throbbed at the heart of her. She wanted, *needed*, so much more. And by the evidence pressing firm and insistent into her belly, he did too. Ciarra rolled her hips and took his growl into her mouth, the deep sound rumbling against her chest from his.

Had she not been a fool, had she not dissolved the one thing in her life that had brought her happiness, their reunion would have been like this. Two halves coming together. Two lovers reunited. Now, she simply stole a moment, hoped to hang on to it for… pain blossomed in her chest. For how long? Would he ever forgive her? Did she even want him to?

Yes.

The truth whispered through her heart. But to ask him, to hope for what may be the impossible, she'd have to admit to a few failures of her own. Ciarra squeezed her eyes tight and focused on the kiss. Later, she would figure out what to say, how to convince him to give her a second chance she didn't deserve. Right at this moment, she wanted to please him. To show him with actions what she couldn't say with words.

She pulled her fingers from his hair and reached between their bodies, seeking out the arousal he couldn't hide. Her fingers closed around his thickness through the fabric and his hips jerked. A sense of anguish at what she couldn't have tightened her muscles and she reached for the buttons of his pants. She needed to taste him. Needed to remember what he sounded like, felt like when she pleasured him in a way she'd always craved, and yet rarely managed to do. He'd have her flat on her back, or on her knees, before she could finish what she started. How desperately she wanted that again. Terran out of control. For her. For them.

Trembling, she popped a button free, then another, before his fingers wrapped around her wrists and stilled her hands. He broke their kiss and leaned his forehead to hers, his breathing heavy, charged with the torment of his restraint.

"Stop, Ciarra," he whispered against her lips. "Not like this."

The trail of hot tears streaming down her cheeks shocked her. When had she started to cry? Caught between mortification and the comfort of his sudden hug, Ciarra fought whether to stay or flee. Oh, summer sun, could she be more pathetic? Once again, he was being the man she remembered, the man she'd fallen in love with. Giving her what she needed because he had the comfort to offer. Unable to resist, she closed her eyes and succumbed to the security of his presence. The rightness of him holding her as if she mattered.

"Why did you give up on us?" he asked softly, his breath fluttering the hair at her ear.

"I was weak," the words broke free before she could

stop the shameful truth. Her breath lodged in her throat. She wanted to be back to what felt good for both of them. Not the heart-crushing admission of her failure. But there was no going back now. Fresh tears tracked a hot path to her jaw.

"I was young, and foolish. Well, younger," she amended, not really sure five years counted a whole lot on the maturity scale in the grand scheme of things. "I was so scared, and my father..."

"Convinced you life with a criminal would not only cost you the Guardianship ranking, but any respect in society," he finished for her.

"He offered to handle the nullifying process for me and," she took a sharp breath, "I let him. I'm coming to the pathetic realization I *always* seem to let him get his way, do what he wants." She pressed her face into his now damp shirt and breathed his masculine scent in deep. A tremor raced through her. Whether at her own disquiet, or the unspent need still filtering through her, she didn't know. "I'm so sorry."

Sighing, he rubbed her back and laid his cheek on top of her head. "I am, too."

Desolation tore a harsh course to her heart. He was... *sorry*. Sorry they couldn't be more. Sorry she'd given up on them. Sorry trust had been shattered. She sniffled. Did she expect something else? Maybe some triumphant declaration of forgiveness? Centering herself, she eased away, trying not to feel more disappointed when he dropped his arms and let her go.

She turned her back to him and swiped her fingers over her cheeks and under her eyes. What was there to say? While he hadn't rejected her, not really, the fist squeezing her heart didn't seem to know the difference.

Movement rustled behind her and when he went back to his lab table, his hair was once again secured neatly behind his neck and his clothes were fixed. The only evidence they'd shared something hot enough to melt ice was the thick bulge in his pants that had yet to settle. Ciarra swallowed and resisted licking her lips. Had she not burst into tears, would he have let her finish what she'd started?

She took a step forward and then stopped. Courage evaded her. All she could think to do now, was somehow figure out a graceful exit. Well, as dignified as she could manage, all things considered. Going to his desk, she found a clean sheet of paper and a pen and returned to her seat across from him.

"Can you give me a quick rundown of patient assessments and virus variants to this point?" she asked, posing her pen for notes.

He arched a brow. "You'll need more than one sheet of paper."

Heat crept along her neck and into her cheeks. Pushing away from the table, she went back and grabbed an empty file and stuffed it full of blank paper. Returning to the stool, she cast an *are you satisfied* stare and waited. A smile tugged at his lips, at least the closest thing to a smile she'd seen since his release.

"I miss your smile," she whispered, and then quickly looked away when she realized she'd said the sentiment out loud.

He shook his head and leaned over the microscope. "Haven't smiled in a long time."

Ciarra knew he left off there'd been no reason for him to be happy. She shoved another wave of guilt aside and forced herself to focus on work. Terran answered her questions with quick efficiency and explained in greater depth when required. She was a long way from her Medical Science Investigator Academia days, and he tended to speak in science rather than Sziverian, as she'd grown accustomed when dealing with cases at Health Services.

What she'd figured would be an easy, quick task stretched until the sun brushed the top of the trees across the field, spearing gold light into the work space. Then again, she mused, as she listened to him dictate his findings from the microscope, she'd fallen back into her assistant role with him. She dutifully wrote his findings on a separate sheet of paper, verbatim, as she'd done so many years before. The ease of their routine had reappeared naturally, comfortably, before either of them had realized, allowing them to get lost in the rhythm of work.

Ciarra's stomach growling finally pulled them from the depths of research. Terran looked up and around, twisting in his seat to take in the vibrant colors of sunset. He rubbed the back of his neck and arched his spine.

"Sorry," he grumbled, rising. "I didn't mean to keep you here all day."

She gathered together all her notes and arranged them neatly in the file, unable to admit out loud she wouldn't have wanted to be anywhere else. "We accomplished a lot."

Shadows gathered in his eyes. "Wish we'd managed more."

Heart in her throat, she waited for him to elaborate. Wondered, if like her, he wanted more. A second chance. He went to the nearest lamp and a match flared in the dimming light.

"I can make us something to eat," he offered, shaking the match out. A wisp of smoke curled in the air near him. "I know you're hungry."

Ciarra let out the breath she hadn't realized she'd been holding. She smiled away disappointment and stood. "No, that's… I'm fine, thanks. I should be getting home anyway."

The cowardice plaguing her didn't suddenly disappear. Nerves didn't spring up, making her find a spine and face him with an overdue apology, and a declaration of the love she should have known would never leave her. Fear of rejection, or even acceptance of her apology, but not her heart, had her fleeing the house with her head held high, once again hiding behind her Shield Guardianess persona.

In her Ariot, she forced the desire to cry away. Resisted the urge to burst back into his house and announce her feelings, regardless of what he decided to do with them. She slammed her hands on the steering column and cursed herself all kinds the fool. Terran was worth fighting for, *they* were worth fighting for. But he held assumptions about her father she wasn't sure she believed. And until she could confirm, or deny, his allegations, they'd stand between them. A battle neither could win.

Scrubbing her hand over her face, she shook off the unfamiliar sensation of weakness. Her drive home was quiet. The roads were uncrowded, the chill of winter still lingering enough to keep people inside once the sun crossed the horizon. Lavender and peach clouds floated in a twilight sky. By the time Ciarra pulled up to her house, stars glittered against the endless black of space.

She stared, leaning against the frame of her vehicle, and wondered if the sky had changed since the cataclysm. Since an event that left most of the world uninhabitable, and those who remained thrown backwards in progress, reverting back to their most basic instincts to survive. If the history books were correct, *survive* may have been an incorrect term, as the Primal Years were aptly named for the period of regression where war and domination ruled.

Resources were still coveted, but thankfully many civilizations had moved forward enough that trade was possible. Progress only moved as fast as the means to create allowed. The vehicle she leaned against was a marvel, a luxury she knew her father had spent more than she thought he'd have. Where had the raimarks come from? She admitted to never having given it much thought until Terran posed the suspicion. Coupled with the other accusations leveled against her father, Ciarra needed answers.

Answers she probably wouldn't receive.

She wasn't stupid. While Byron felt his daughter capable of running Health Services, it was only because *he* had placed her there. Ciarra was, and always would be, beneath him in his eyes. A young woman who would still be learning her ways until the day he passed. Ciarra sighed, and file in hand, went into the warm house. Somehow, she'd have to figure out how to find the truth on her own.

The thought of investigating her father made her a little queasy. Despite his flaws, he loved her, had cared for her in his own way when her mother had left them instead of remaining in Sziveria for the mandatory contract length of eighteen years after Ciarra's birth. Ciarra had tried not to take the abandonment personally. Her father had pointed out when she was older however, that while neither of her parents could have contracted again, he wouldn't have forced her mother to stay in the same room with him, let alone the same home. She could have remained, could have helped him raise her, living separately. But she hadn't. Where Margie Jonatis ended up, Ciarra never learned. So no, she didn't want to think the worst of her only parent. Didn't want to consider he could be capable of something as horrible as purposefully infecting citizens with a deadly contagion.

Yet, the city, possibly the whole of Sziveria, couldn't afford Ciarra's discomfort at discovering the truth. The betrayal of such an undertaking would likely be the end of her relationship with the dowager Levkaseon. Ciarra would cross such a road when the moment arrived. For the time being, she'd deal with one disaster at a time.

No lamps burned in the entry hall. No fires warmed the downstairs. Sighing, Ciarra made her way into the depths of the house through the darkness to the library. Folders still sat stacked haphazardly where her father had left them the night before. She tried not to think about all the hours she'd waste digging through them to find the information Terran had asked. He needed a timeline, starting before the evident mini-epidemic, to gauge the actual change in patterns. Had Byron not messed with her work, the task would have been fairly simple. Now? She grumbled as she set the new file down. The job would be trickier.

After lighting a fire to ward off the cold, and lamps

to see by, she settled behind her desk and went to work. Hours later, her stomach once again protested neglect, and finally made her stop. The dark kitchen offered little for her scrounge up without cooking, which she didn't know how to do. She managed to find some bread, cheese, an orange, and snagged a handful of cookies, piling it all on a plate and taking it back to the library. Starving, she munched on an orange wedge, juice dribbling down her chin, as she strode back into the room.

Her eyes landed on dark shadows flowing through the room like wraiths and she skidded to a stop. One moved to her desk. Another black form shuffled through her things. Several files were tossed to another shadowy figure, papers flying free. Without pausing to see what had been thrown, the intruder flung the file into the fire. The third invader picked up an armload of cases and followed suit, throwing the whole bunch into the popping flames. Shocked at her work being burned, she choked on a gasp, the plate slipping from her fingers.

The three froze. Fury erupted inside her. Not thinking beyond interrupting them from wrecking further havoc on information she couldn't afford to lose, she reached along the nearest shelf. Her fingers touched a cold bronze statuette and she gripped it tight. A quick glance showed her the closest villain and with a scream of anger, she launched the heavy object.

"Get out of my house!" she roared, and searched for another weapon.

Smooth cold stone met her touch and she didn't even look, just grabbed and sent the art soaring toward another body. The aim hit true, catching the one nearest to the fireplace in the shoulder. He stumbled, lost his balance, and crashed into the bookshelves. The force of his fall sent books and trinkets raining down on his head. Ciarra lobbed items as fast as she could reach while the other two wraiths ducked.

"Out!" she demanded again.

Before she could launch another assault, one of the intruders barreled into her. A man by the weight and density. She flew backwards, landing hard on her butt, her shoulders slamming into the wooden floor. The man sprawled on top of her. He recovered quicker than her. Straddling her hips, his powerful thighs kept the lower half of her body immobile while he made an attempt to grab her forearms. Panic sleuthed through Ciarra. She slapped, bucked, and made as much noise as possible, wondering how to this point no one had heard her. Their staff didn't live in a separate building, but they did reside in a separate wing. Sound traveled though, and she'd made plenty.

"Where's that damn rope?" her captor asked, his deep voice strained.

Rope? Oh no. Ciarra doubled her efforts. No way was she going to be tied up in her own home. He finally grabbed hold of one her arms and yanked, forcing her at an odd angle on a cry. The leverage was what he needed and on another harsh jerk, he made her twist onto her stomach. Pain erupted in her shoulder and the small of her back. He dug his knee deep into the tail of her spine until she screamed. His elbow landed on her jaw, shoving her head down onto the floor.

"Shut it!" he hissed. "The rope!"

"Just leave her, we're done here," someone

answered, the voice lighter, softer. Either a younger male or a woman.

He ground his forearm into her cheek and jaw harshly before vaulting off her. Shoulder on fire, and a spasming ache in her back had Ciarra moving much slower. The echo of running boots and the slamming of a door followed by silence told her she was alone. At least, she hoped she was. Laying her palms flat, she pushed up with a groan. Her back and shoulder protested the movement. She panted through the discomfort and surveyed the disaster.

Flames licked and snapped in the fireplace, devouring the remains of curling pages and file folders. The objects she'd lobbed littered the floor, along with random sheets that had fluttered free. Her entire desk had been cleared. An overturned chair and the trail of documents to the fireplace showed the rush to kick what could be destroyed into the fire. Ciarra sat back on her hunches and sniffled. Using the bookshelf, she hauled herself up.

The calm stillness of the house contrasted the pounding rush of blood in her ears. Where had everyone gone? And where was her father? Surely, he'd heard the commotion. Ciarra blinked and then sprinted from the room. She took the stairs two at a time and ran down the hall, using the wall to keep herself upright when a throbbing twinge in her back almost sent her to her knees. How hard had the scab needed to kneel on her? The yawning darkness of her father's open bedroom door had her slowing. He never kept his door open.

"Father?" she called out.

She slowed when she reached his door, using her

fingertips to push it open further. No light shone from the pellet stove, or a lamp. She felt along the wall nearest to the door for an oil lamp and lit one. The pale glow illuminated a tidy room. The bed was still made with light blue silk pajamas laid out neatly in the center. Ciarra frowned and pressed a hand to her chest, where a painful knot had formed. For some reason she'd been left completely alone in the house, and her work destroyed.

Backing out of her father's room, she turned, trying not to hyperventilate. In a daze of confusion bordering on panic, Ciarra stumbled back downstairs. Maybe he was in his lab. He'd been known to get caught up in work. Though, not so much recently with his illness. That would explain why he hadn't heard her. She went down the narrow staircase and tested the doorknob. The door swung open, and like his bedroom, revealed a dark, empty space.

"Okay," she whispered and eased back up the stairs. "Okay, I'm completely alone."

She ran to her room, terror nipping at her heels. The need to get out of the house bordered on all consuming. She searched her closet for a bag, a box, anything to shove incidentals in. No way was she remaining any longer than it took to pack enough to stay somewhere safe. Anger flared at being forced out of her home. To be intruded upon in such a way that the one place considered secure above all others had been violated.

Every stray creak and rustle made her jump and then freeze, straining to hear over her thundering pulse. The second she had enough stuffed into a canvas bag to survive a few days, she grabbed the stiff woven handles and hefted it over her shoulder. Downstairs, she checked in the library to make sure none of the burning papers had managed to throw an ember and set fire to the room. She dithered, and then closed the grate across the fireplace, ensuring the dying ashes stayed contained.

At the front door, she paused, her hand hovering over the handle. What if someone waited outside? Then again, the intruder had stated they were finished. They'd come to destroy her work, and they'd succeeded. Steeling her nerves, Ciarra opened the door. Cold air swept past, fluttering her hair. The nights hadn't warmed enough for life, which only chirped, croaked and warbled for a few precious months. Unnerved by the silence, Ciarra took a deep breath and forced herself to step outside. She ran to the Ariot. She threw the bag onto the passenger seat as she slammed the door.

Paranoid, she drove around the city, making random turns, careful to stay where she was familiar with every side road and alley. She avoided glistening patches of ice and kept a cautious watch at each stop to make sure she wasn't being followed. As she wove a seemingly random path through Haven City, she considered where to go. A hotel would be the smartest, but as a Shield Guardian, a lot of questions would be asked. She'd be lucky if her overnight adventure didn't make *The Havener* come morning.

Ciarra turned another corner, wishing she'd taken the time to make more friends. As it was, she didn't have any she felt comfortable enough to possibly put in some sort of danger and be forgiven. The only remaining place was Terran's. And he couldn't really get any angrier with her, she figured. Fighting the inevitable was useless, so after she was positive no one followed, she steered in the direction of his house.

Patches of ice glowed in the moonlight. She carefully avoided them, having to slow some as the city faded. Terran's drive came into view, and she pulled down the long stretch, stopping at what she'd come to think of as her spot in front of the greenhouse. The panes of glass shimmered in the silvery light, while the metal frame looked almost skeletal. She'd barely disengaged the engine when a glow cut across the drive from the interior. Light arched around Terran's large frame taking up the entrance, making him a hulking shadow.

"What happened?" he asked the second she stepped foot onto the gravel.

She had to swallow several times before the words unstuck from her throat. "Someone came into my home and destroyed all my work. Threw it the fireplace. My father..." She took a slow breath. "My father is missing."

TERRAN FORCED HIMSELF TO STAY STILL, TO REMAIN IN THE doorway and not rush to her side. The distress in her voice called to the primal side of his being, the one who still looked at her and saw his wife. She pulled a bag from the vehicle, and he stared. That could only mean one thing. Ciarra meant to stay in his house. With him. Overnight.

He needed to focus on the important part of her words. "Are you okay?"

"I'm fine. Shaken, but fine." She stopped in front of him and shook her head. "They destroyed *everything*."

Terran relieved her of the bag and ushered her into

the safety of the warm house in front of him. "Everything can be redrafted. You, however, can't be replaced."

She shot him a veiled glance over her shoulder, blinked, and then continued on. "I'm worried about my father."

A snort escaped before he could contain the sarcastic reaction. Shadows crossed her face, adding to the lines of fatigue. Clearly, she was at the end of her tolerance, and he hadn't helped matters. Terran held a hand out while closing the door. "I'm sorry, that was uncalled for."

Sighing, she shook her head. "No, I know how you feel." In the barren, open living space, she stopped and turned to face him, not bothering to hide her worry. "It's just, I know my father loves me. I know he's made some terrible choices, I can't ignore that anymore, but after my mother left us..." She looked away. "He did what he thought was right."

"I don't know." Terran said softly. "I'm positive some of the decisions he knew were very wrong."

She rubbed her arms. "Perhaps."

Terran ran his free hand down his face and echoed her earlier sigh. "Did it look as if he'd been taken against his will?"

"No. Though, I don't know where he'd go. He never leaves the house anymore. He's too sick. The cold irritates his lungs," she answered, looking around as if searching for something.

She appeared lost, small. Terran kept his distance. The last time he'd offered her comfort had been a near disaster. He didn't think he'd be able to stop anything from happening again, so best to make sure nothing started to begin with.

He waved to the lone chair in front of the fireplace. "You're welcome to sit."

"Can we walk in the greenhouse?"

Terran looked to the black windows and frowned. "I haven't tended to the overgrowth, yet."

"Oh that's right." She chuckled and a small smile toyed at her lips. "Falling in the dark may be more disastrous than during the day. You may never find me."

Her shoulders sagged and she squeezed her eyes shut.

"You're exhausted," he said.

"Adrenaline let down," she clarified.

He frowned. "Did you ever manage to eat anything?"

She rubbed her hands on her thighs. "I was carrying food in when I caught them."

"I'm going to take this up and then I'll make you something."

"Terran—"

"No. No arguing. You need to eat and relax and then go rest. Tomorrow promises to be an interesting day, which you won't be able to take on exhausted and starved." He waited for her to argue again, but her shoulders slouched further and she nodded. "Good."

He went upstairs and tossed her bag onto the mattress. Since he only had one in the house, he'd have to figure something out. No way was he risking sleeping in the same bed as her. Too many vivid memories of waking in the middle of the night, with her soft skin under his palm and her body responding to his every touch. One sleepy caress and they'd both be sunk, pulled under by the weight of their desire.

Yes, he could admit to himself he wanted her. Desperately. What he didn't want was another punch to the gut and his heart ripped from his chest. Part of him argued he could deliver an ultimatum. A quick relationship that ended with the threat. But he knew it would never be enough. Not for him, not for her. So, he needed a different stipulation. He shook his head and growled at his wayward thoughts. Anything else would require trust. Even if he asked for a year contract, a chance for them to see if they could make things work again, he'd have to trust she'd honor even the year.

Terran didn't know what was going to happen tomorrow, let alone a year from now. Voklane had sworn Terran wouldn't be sent back to prison, but how much power did the unranked Guardian really have? Could he even ask for a year, not knowing if he would be around to see it through, either? None of the options seemed fair, or viable. Which meant he needed to keep his distance.

The quiet downstairs made him pause on the steps. Ciarra must have finally slowed down enough to sit. He found her sound asleep in the chair. For quiet minutes, he allowed himself the simple pleasure of watching her. Beautiful wasn't an accurate enough word to describe how she looked to him. An ache wrapped around his heart.

He missed her.

So much.

How was it possible to miss someone not feet away? Scrubbing his hands down his face, he debated waking her so she could eat, or taking her upstairs to sleep somewhere more comfortable. She probably wouldn't eat much if she was so exhausted, she crashed in the sorry excuse for a chair Voklane had planted in the living room. Terran would just have to make sure he fed her a really good breakfast. He gathered her into his arms. The unconscious weight of her flopped against his chest. Her head settled into the crook of his neck, her warm breath teasing his skin. Cautiously, he took the stairs, aware with each sought out step the precious cargo in his hold if he were to slip.

In his room, he gently laid her on the bed, folding the covers back before settling and covering her. On a soft sigh, she snuggled into the pillow, wrapping the blankets tight around herself. He couldn't help but smile. She'd always been a blanket thief. A lock of golden hair fell over her cheek, and he smoothed it back into place, his fingers lingering in the silken depths.

Before he could resist the urge, he leaned down and pressed a kiss to her temple. She murmured and shifted, her mouth too close to ignore. Terran whispered a kiss across hers and traced his thumb along her bottom lip. "Good night, my Ciarra."

8

The rich aroma of bacon, coffee and something sweet pulled Ciarra from sleep. She stretched, her eyes fluttering open. Bright light glowed along the seams of the drawn navy brocade curtains. Rolling onto her stomach, she buried her face deep into the fluffy pillow and breathed deep. Terran's scent infused her nostrils and her body hummed awake for a whole different reason.

Pushing onto her elbows, Ciarra groaned at the aches reminding her of the short-lived adventure from the night before and blew tangled hair from her face. She took in the messy bed and the lack of evidence that she'd shared the mattress. Where had Terran slept? She rose to her knees, frowning. The blankets fell away, leaving her chilled. Yesterday's clothing hung in a rumpled mess on her body. On her haunches, she heaved a long sigh and considered her options. Shower and present herself in a manner that would ensure her confidence, or... or remind him she'd once been allowed to be vulnerable. Messy.

Completely herself around him. Maybe she needed such a reminder, too.

While sitting alone last night, with only her thoughts for company, she'd had to admit she'd never stopped loving Terran. The realization hadn't been the shock she'd expected. Rather a slow, easy turn of her heart and a sense of anticipation at a future they may still have a chance to unfold. Despite having every right to his anger, he'd taken her in, sheltered her, held her when she needed comfort. Prison may have changed him outwardly, but deep inside he was still the same kind, caring man she'd fallen hard for and had been denied learning so much more about. A plan formulated in her mind, making her heart thump heavy in her chest. Yes. She could do this.

Decision made, Ciarra crawled off the bed, went into the bathroom, brushed her teeth and ignored her crazy hair. After drying her hands and face, she went downstairs. A nervous flutter danced in her belly. The chance he'd reject her proposal was high. Not that she could blame him. Trust wasn't something she'd earned yet, and wouldn't until he let her.

The crackle of bacon accompanied the clatter of a pan. His broad back was to her. The thin sage green knit sweater he wore fitted to his shoulders and upper arms, accentuating the play of muscles with each move he made. He'd pulled back the sides of his long hair, but left the rest to fall freely to his shoulders. The bright morning sun caught on the lighter strands as he shifted from one part of the kitchen to another. When he noticed her, he paused, his head jerking back slightly in reaction.

Ciarra smiled. She figured her disheveled appearance caused his awkward response. Her stomach growled. "I'm starving," she said by way of excuse.

"Ah," he said, holding a finger up. He spun around, grasped a plate and set it on the bar across from him. "You can grab a chair from the lab, or even eat in there, if you prefer."

"With the virus for company?" She laughed and finished walking into the kitchen. "No thanks."

"It can't hurt you," he said softly.

Ciarra tucked unruly locks of hair behind her ears and surveyed the bountiful meal before her. A heap of bacon, scrambled eggs, orange slices and fluffy sweet fried bread beckoned her. "We aren't all immune, like you. Just being in the same room requires a real effort to keep from panicking at times."

He handed her a fork, the silver flashing as he set it on the plate. "Well, I destroyed the samples I took, I was done with them. With you in the house, I couldn't risk someone getting stupid in the lab."

Ciarra paused, the fork stuck in the fluffy eggs. "You think someone followed me? I tried to make sure no one did."

"I'm not willing to risk it," he clarified, holding a hand up. "I'm not upset. I'm glad you came, that you trusted me enough to feel safe here. I don't think anyone followed you, nor could they possibly know where I'm living. Not yet. That doesn't mean my location will stay secret for long. If someone destroyed your research, they'll be after mine next."

Frowning, she poked at her food. "What a mess."

"I didn't expect anything else," he admitted, turning back to his cooking. "Eat, before it gets any colder."

The buttery, perfectly cooked eggs took her by

surprise. Her shock must have shown, for Terran laughed. Ciarra flushed and ducked her head, focusing on the sweet bread. "I wasn't aware you could cook."

"I was passable before prison." He removed the sizzling bacon from the stove, setting it on a folded towel on the counter. "Learning to feed fellow prisoners well ensured I didn't get messed with too often."

She peeled the rind off her orange slice. "I figured your talent would have kept them away from you. After all, I don't think anyone else could save their life quite like you could."

"Unless you're dying, you don't really care who could possibly save you in the future. But a full belly?" He lifted a slice of perfectly cooked crispy bacon and took a bite. "Everyone cares about that."

"Were you... messed with... often?" she asked, almost afraid of the answer.

"Ashen Shores was an ocean side correction facility. Honestly, I couldn't have been confined to a better location. The Master Guardian in charge gave each inmate one pass at misbehavior, after that," he hitched a thumb over his shoulder, "you were gone. No second chances. He liked peace and quiet, and as a reward we had beach time once a week when the weather allowed."

"He wasn't worried about anyone swimming away?"

"This wasn't the Sovereign Channel, where the warmer air makes the water more tolerable. You could *maybe* go fifteen minutes in the summer before turning blue. In the spring or fall? Forget it. Sometimes chunks of ice still floated to shore." He lifted his face and breathed in deep. "But on the beach? With the wind, the sun or even the rain, the waves, and the birds, for that little bit of time, I could almost forget I was locked away."

The compulsion to go to him, to smooth the strain of bad memories from his face, had Ciarra gripping the edge of her plate. "Sounds peaceful."

"It was," he agreed and began to clean up the kitchen. "Which is why Ashen Shores is one of the safest facilities in Sziveria. No one wants to leave to serve their sentence anywhere else."

And what was Ciarra supposed to say to that? *I'm so glad you were in a nice prison…?* She watched him wash the dishes, using a soapy washcloth to scrub the plates and pans clean. "Will you ever hire someone to help you?"

He glanced up before returning to his chore. "We already discussed this. No, a stranger won't be coming to my home, let alone living with me."

Ciarra considered his words and tried not to be horrified. She figured, over time, he'd change his mind. However, the ease with which he cleaned the kitchen made his decision clear. He didn't mind picking up after himself, or doing the menial, everyday tasks she couldn't imagine, let alone complete.

"I can barely brush my own hair," she admitted, thinking about all the tasks he had to do on a daily basis. "I don't even choose the clothes I'm going to wear for the day."

He shook water off the last plate and then set it in some sort of drying rack on the counter next to the sink with the other dishes. "I guess it's a good thing you aren't stuck here then, isn't it?"

Now or never, she figured. Either she had the guts to forge forward and speak her mind, or she didn't deserve the man standing in front of her. Not that she did anyway. However, she'd never know if they had a chance, even a small one, if she didn't ask. She took a shaky breath and drew imaginary, random shapes on the marble counter with her index finger.

"What if I wanted to?" she asked slowly, and then clarified, "Be stuck here."

TERRAN STILLED. EVEN HIS BREATHING SLOWED. HE watched Ciarra carefully, trying to decide if she were joking or completely serious. Unsure which one he actually wanted of the two. The burst of hope, and excitement at her words, had him fighting anger, more with himself than at her obvious interest in a future *she'd* been the one to throw away. Because here he stood, really considering saying yes. Wanting to with a desire that made him turn away so he couldn't see the same hope reflected in her eyes.

The brush of her fingers on his sleeve at his elbow had him squeezing his eyes closed. "Why?" he asked, more in a growl than anything comprehensive.

"Could I say anything that would convince you I'm being honest?"

The tremble in her voice made him glance down at her. "I don't know. Try me and see."

She swallowed and smoothed a tousled lock of hair behind her ear. No denying, the woman was a mess. Her clothes were wrinkled, the shirt hung lopsided like she'd pulled one side straight in her sleep, while the other crinkled in on itself. The faded smudges of black under her eyes showed evidence that she'd tried to wash her face, but hadn't completely been able to get rid of yesterday's makeup. She didn't look like a Shield Guardianess. No, she looked like *his* Ciarra. Not afraid to be seen by the man she loved, because he could never love her less.

"Do you remember our promising ceremony? Where we promised to stand together no matter how difficult the next ten years were? To not pressure the other to begin a family before either of us were ready? Or when we promised to be honest because most fights are based on misunderstandings?" she asked, turning to face the wide windows in the dining nook.

"Yes, how could I forget?" The anticipation, the excitement, the wonder of a new relationship and the promises they'd carefully prepared for each other to be fulfilled over the coming years. Only to be shattered six short months later by her father. Anger, thick and poisonous, threatened the fragile truce she was attempting to build between them. He willed the damaging reaction away.

She took a deep breath. "Right. Well, I was twenty-two when we made those promises, and I was still twenty-two when my father saw to them being broken." She turned to face him, her fingers bunched in the silk of her shirt. "See, I made the mistake of thinking *he* would honor our promises, too. And when he didn't, I didn't think I had much power to oppose him. I know it's not a strong excuse, and I know I made zero effort to learn the truth. I trusted him implicitly."

Her hands splayed open in supplication. Tears shimmered in the beautiful depths of her stormy gray eyes. "I made a mistake. A huge one. And... I'm sorry. I know it'll never be enough, how could anything I say ever be enough?" A tear rolled down her cheek and dripped from her jaw. "But I am. I am so very sorry."

Terran's chest constricted, and he struggled to breathe. Oh, summer sun, how he wanted to believe her. Second chances were a rare, beautiful thing. So far, he'd been given two, one for his life, and another for his career. Ciarra offered another opportunity to reclaim what had been taken from him. Their relationship.

All he had to do was forgive.

A simple word for a not so simple feat.

"Terran, speak to me, please," she implored, his silence seeming to unnerve her.

He scrubbed his hands down his face. "Where do you see this going? What exactly do you want from me?"

"I don't know." She shrugged. "I figured I'd let you set the parameters."

Terran bit back a sarcastic retort. Picking a fight would undo everything she was trying, and he had no doubt she was indeed *trying*, to accomplish. He clasped his hands behind his neck and stretched back, looking up into the vaulted rafters of the house. "What about your father? How will he play into your plans? And since he had the power to send me to prison before, he might be able to do so again. What then?" A fist clenched in his stomach. "I can't go through that again, I won't. If I leave the country, would you go with me?"

"Well," she began slowly, "aside from finding my father? He won't have anything to do with our relationship. I made a mistake when I allowed the concession to begin with. As for leaving if we must? Yes. Isn't that the point of this, to stand together no matter what this time?"

Terran continued to stare at the ceiling, allowing the spark of hope to thaw the ice around his heart. He couldn't stop a chuckle from escaping. "I don't think any of that will go over well with him."

"Probably not."

"And you'll accept his wrath?" he asked, crossing his arms over his chest and meeting her gaze. "You'll handle whatever anger he directs your way? He has the power to threaten to remove your Guardianship from you, and actually succeed."

Her chin lifted. "Then it was never my Guardianship to begin with, was it?"

"I suppose not," he agreed softly.

She sniffled and looked away. "Besides, I'm fairly certain if what you suspect is true, I'll lose the rank anyway."

Terran shifted his weight back until he leaned against the counter. "Even though I'm working for the FIO right now, I'm not ranked. I don't even know if an accused can hold a ranking."

"You think I care about that?"

He shrugged again. "I have no idea, Ciarra. It's the only life you've ever known. I imagine the thought of being outside of a society you were raised in would be somewhat unsettling."

Looking away from him, she pulled her bottom lip into her mouth. "No more so than believing my father is capable of betrayal."

Terran didn't just believe, he knew firsthand the bite of Byron's treachery. "Okay, so that leaves the parameters as you say."

She nodded but remained silent.

"No promise ceremony, because there won't be a

point. I want for life, kids or not. You want to do this again, then you'll trust me, and we do it all the way. No testing the waters, no wondering if we'll still want each other in a decade, or whatever. We'll make it work, or we decide we won't."

"A contract," she said carefully, "for life."

"Yes."

Aside from losing a little color, she didn't flee. She took a measured breath and released it just as gradually. "Okay, why?"

"Because anything less isn't long enough," he answered with honesty. "I need to know you trust in *us* enough to go all in."

The sheen of tears returned to her eyes. "Even though I hurt you?"

Straightening from the counter, Terran reached for her. He wrapped his fingers around the back of her neck and pulled her close, resting their foreheads together. "That's the thing about forgiveness. I can either let the past control me, or I can let it go and heal. With you."

"You really forgive me?" she asked, her voice small, unsteady.

Warmth spread through Terran. Five years he'd been deprived of the feeling of comfort and happiness. The tiny seed she'd planted with her earlier declaration had already grown, sprouted and spawned a leaf from which to build and nurture. "Are you really giving me your heart again?"

Her hands wrapped around his forearms and squeezed. "I feel like that's a question I should be asking."

"Ciarra, don't," he whispered, pressing a gentle kiss

to her lips. He hated the flash of vulnerability at her query. "I don't know if I'm ready to answer that yet."

Her eyes squeezed closed. "But you're ready to be with me forever?"

"Yes, and my heart will be along for the journey, only yours to claim."

"Fair enough. Will you give me your name?"

Unsure if he'd heard her correctly, he leaned back and stared down at her. "Taking my name will mean your father won't have to threaten to take anything. You'll lose your ranking."

She closed her eyes and released a slow breath between pursed lips. "I know. But I can't ask you to take mine again, and I won't have us living under different names. If we're to be together, then it's united, in everything. Right? That's what you've been saying?" Another trembling sigh escaped her. "Besides, I'm not so sure I want to be a Jonatis anymore, either. I don't want to believe he's done something so awful, but I'm so scared it's too late and he already has."

Terran held the same concern, minus the doubt. Still, he didn't understand why she'd give up something so important. "Why would you willingly give up being a Shield Guardian?"

She swallowed and tried to pull away from him, but he tightened his hold and pulled her closer. Tentatively, she lifted her gaze to his. "I never really wanted to be Levkaseon to begin with. My father was so obsessed with keeping the rank in our family, that when I turned twenty-six and still had yet to produce an heir, he started trying to pressure me into another contract. But I was older, and… and none of them were you."

The burn of possession should have taken him by

surprise, considering how long he'd held onto his bitterness. But the feeling of Ciarra being his had hounded him since he'd seen her step from the Ariot five days ago. She'd never *stopped* being his. A truth he'd been refusing to acknowledge, shoving it deep. Now, called forward, he couldn't ignore the ache to make her his again. To be part of something special. Unique.

"You won't be anyone else's," he growled.

"And neither will you," she said, her hands sliding up his arms to grip his shoulders.

Inevitable, and oh so necessary, his lips descended on hers in a claiming kiss. She opened without hesitation, accepting his onslaught, submitting to his demand. Terran spun them around and lifted her onto the counter. With a little wiggle, she scooted to the edge, driving him insane as she positioned herself perfectly to take advantage of him standing between her now parted thighs. Her boldness didn't shock him. Ciarra had always known what she wanted as a lover, and was never shy in taking, or even asking.

She tasted of oranges and sugar and he couldn't get enough. His mouth slanted over hers again and again. Savored every sleek texture. Explored all the hidden surfaces that made her moan, made her arch into him to pursue more. Kneading his fingers into the supple flesh of her hips, he flexed against her. Pleasure sizzled along his nerves and urged him to continue. She hugged him close until only clothes kept them apart.

He slipped under the hem of her shirt. The warmth of her skin met his fingers. If he focused his talent, he could see the healthy blood cells rushing through her system. An impulse he used to give in to often. Either because he dealt in death more than life, and knowing she was healthy and safe brought him relief, or because he couldn't resist being that much closer to her. He figured probably a mixture of both. The only reason he resisted now was because she still had all her clothes on and he wasn't buried deep inside her. She tugged his shirt up, her touch fluttering across the tensed muscles of his stomach and to the waist of his pants.

Her mouth pulled free as she leaned back, sliding his shirt further up. Like a caress, her gaze shifted over his exposed skin. "Wow," she breathed, spanning her hands along his flanks. "You're so different... from before."

"In many ways," he agreed. "Do you need time?"

"Time?" she asked distractedly.

"To get to know me better before we sign the contract?" He brushed his lips along her neck to her collar bone. Freesia and the sleepy scent of his sheets surrounded him.

Her hands slipped beneath the waist of his pants to grip his lower hips. "No. I know the most important things about you. The rest?" She shrugged and stroked her warm fingers up his back. "I can't wait to learn."

Terran captured her mouth again, silencing her words that threatened to unraveled the last strings of his control. She met his passion head on, adding to their fire. Too unsettled to bother attempting with the row of buttons on the front of her shirt, he yanked. The thread gave and buttons popped and bounced around them on the counter and the floor.

Ciarra gasped, but leaned back, giving him the access he desperately wanted to her breasts. Her fingers threaded into his hair, pulling on the bound strands. He bit and licked all the way to one nipple, pulling the tight bud into his mouth and sucking hard, like he remembered her enjoying. She arched, his name a cry and plea all at the same time. Impatient to know how much she wanted him, he fumbled with the clasp of her pants.

A heavy *bang, bang, bang* echoed through the house. They both froze. The demanding pounding sounded again. Terran straightened and spun away from her. Desire would have to wait. Only one other person knew where he lived. Behind him, Ciarra's feet slapped on the marble tiles. He glanced over his shoulder and a new rush of heat flowed through his veins. She clutched the now ruined shirt between her breasts. Her lips were swollen, her hair a disaster. There was no mistaking what they'd been doing. Yet she walked with confidence and authority, as if they had every right to the passion they'd almost given into, and the embarrassment of the interruption was best left to the person who'd brought their moment to an end.

Terran unlocked the door and yanked it open. Harsh morning sun nearly blinded him, though not even the brilliant light had removed the chill of night. Stepping back, he took in Ryan Voklane's frown. "Trouble?"

"A bit," Ryan admitted and shouldered his way inside. He nodded to Ciarra, unphased by her disheveled state. "Shield Guardianess Levkaseon."

"Guardian Voklane," she replied without hesitation.

Terran closed the door. "Is there time for Ciarra to dress?"

"There will be," Ryan said. "Nine HRS incidents happened this morning, all on the street, and six magic lily dust overdoses."

Ciarra muttered a rare curse. Without another word, she raced up the stairs. Terran gestured deeper into the house.

"I have some breakfast left, if you're hungry," Terran offered.

Ryan sighed and rubbed his fingers across his forehead. "I could eat, thanks."

Grabbing a clean plate from the drying rack, Terran loaded it with cooling bacon and a few pieces of sweet fry bread and sliced oranges. He slid the dish to Ryan across the spacious bar. Ryan took the food and then glanced around.

"Why don't you have anything to sit on?" the FIO Guardian asked.

Terran arched a brow and stared.

Ryan closed his eyes and chuckled under his breath. "Right. Sorry."

"You can eat in the lab or standing up."

Without another word, Voklane carried the meal into the lab. He sat at Terran's desk, taking a quick look around before diving into the meal. "Nice set up."

Terran shoved his hands into his pockets and rocked back on his heels. "Thanks for all the supplies."

Bacon crunched before Ryan answered. "You should have asked for more."

"You managed to get me this massive house, outside the city, and a fully furnished lab and an entire wardrobe. Far more than I expected."

"Less than you were owed," Ryan stated, his pale silvery-blue eyes serious. "I have a radio in my Ariot for you."

"Thank you," Terran said with a small smile. "I

imagine having to come all the way out here to fetch us was inconvenient."

Ryan shook his head. "You fed me, so the drive was worth it. But I said I'd get you one, so I did."

Terran laughed. "Okay." He grabbed a stool from in front of the last microscope he'd been using and carried it closer to the desk. "Someone destroyed all of Ciarra's work in her house last night."

Ryan stopped with a bite of bread halfway to his mouth. "Well, isn't that familiar."

Sighing, Terran rubbed the back of his neck. "Yeah, little bit. Byron wasn't home, either."

"No one was home," Ciarra said from the doorway. She carried the boots she'd been wearing last night in her hand. A flowy, long sleeve red silk tunic fluttered as she walked, pairing elegantly with equally loose black fine spun wool slacks. "I was alone."

Anger flashed through Terran at her statement, given coolly, as though being left at the hands of intruders were no big deal. "Everyone in the house was gone?"

She braced her lower back on the edge of a table and pulled on a boot. "Either that, or they ignored my shouts."

Ryan shifted in his seat. "But you weren't hurt?"

"Not really, no." She kept her head down as she pulled on her other shoe.

"Meaning?" Terran asked. She'd fallen asleep before he'd been able to find out everything that had happened. And this morning... Well, they'd had an entirely different distraction.

Straightening, she brushed hair from her face. "Meaning they finished what they'd been sent to do and I wasn't their problem anymore." She turned her attention to Ryan. "Have you heard anything about my father?"

"No," Ryan answered.

Ciarra released a breath. "Well, I guess that's good. He won't be waiting for me in the morgue."

"No," Ryan said, his frown deepening. "Your morgue is plenty full enough."

9

THE ECHO OF THEIR STEPS WAS THE ONLY SOUND IN THE morgue corridor. Ciarra pulled her white work coat tighter across her shoulders and tried to dispel the odd, unwelcome nervousness fluttering in her stomach. Following a few steps behind were Terran and Voklane. This was her domain, for a little while longer. No one had unseated her yet, or discovered a true link between her father and whatever happened in the city concerning the rabies virus. She had nothing to be worried about. However, she wasn't so naïve as to realize the truth would be exposed. Soon, if Terran had his way.

The morning threatened to break her concentration from what was important, to what was to come. Marriage. Her plan to convince him to give her a second chance produced results well beyond her greatest imaginings. And she'd been imagining a whole lot when it came to Terran. Glancing sideways, she took in his fit, confident form. Yeah. Lots.

If not for the interruption, no doubt they'd have

sealed their declaration for a future together in a very pleasurable way. She knew how his mind worked. To him, they'd already declared the intent, their marriage was as good as finalized. They just needed a legal record for the government, not for themselves. Butterflies danced in her stomach. She would have accepted the minimum year for a legal union, anything to be with him again, but he wanted forever. He didn't even need the security the contract was meant to provide since he couldn't become contagious with, or pass on, the HRS virus. And still, he wanted her as his wife. Ciarra pressed her lips together to keep from smiling. Not the time, or the place.

Little red flags lined the hall from the right of each doorframe, indicating the room had a body waiting for examination. If what Ryan had said was true, sixteen of the twenty exam rooms held a body. They could double up, if necessary. Each room had two cold storage units. Swinging doors slapped open down at the other end. White light spilled into the space before long shadows and garbled voices. Wheels squeaked. Two men pushed a covered gurney to the first room without a flag. Ciarra picked up the pace.

Inside the room, they positioned the gurney and locked the wheels. One of the attendants, a young man with *Gregory* sewn onto his dark blue shirt, clipped a board with documents onto the end of the metal table. The other, wearing the same type of clothes, taller and a little older, signed something and deposited the paper in a tray next to the door. They noticed her at the same time and fell silent. Ciarra went to the clipboard.

"Gentlemen," she acknowledged.

"Shield Guardianess," they said in unison.

She read over the basic report and then handed the information over to Terran. "Are any more arriving?"

Gregory shrugged. "We don't have anyone else to bring in, no, but it's been a crazy day so far."

"Yeah, we're earning our pay today," the other man said with a sad shake of his head.

Ciarra thanked them and waited until they exited before pulling down the sheet. A young woman, gray in death, her chin, neck and the entire front of her floral print gown glistened with saliva and drying blood. An HRS victim, not an overdose.

"Make that ten," Voklane stated grimly.

Terran lifted the sheet until he uncovered a portion of the woman not soiled by bodily fluids. He touched the inside of her calf, eyes closed, face set in concentration. "Not the original virus."

"Okay." Ciarra grounded her thoughts and turned to the work table. The timeline she'd been working on for Terran before the intruders had destroyed her hard work was still fairly fresh in her mind. She grasped a form and flipped it over to a blank back. She divided the paper. "We know for certain there were three HRS incidents nine days ago based on the positive patient at the containment facility. Those three patients were infected with the original virus."

Terran went to the sink to wash his hands. "Correct. And none of them bit anyone?"

Ciarra shook her head. "No, they were each contained after going active without casualties."

"What about before that?" Ryan asked, coming to stand beside the desk.

Ciarra shrugged. "I don't know. We didn't have Terran before that."

"But there were still cluster incidents, right?"

"Yes, it's what prompted me to ask for his release," Ciarra replied.

"And aside from the one living case, I haven't seen an original strain of the virus," Terran stated, drying his hands.

Ciarra's chest constricted. "That's a lot of mutated strain cases," she whispered.

"That aren't contagious, and are rapid acting," Terran said.

Ryan ran a hand down his face. "All right, so if they aren't contagious, how are the victims getting infected to begin with?"

Terran went to the victim. "I'll handle her autopsy, see what I can find. If anything turns up, I'll check the others."

Concentrating on the timeline, she wrote out everything she could remember over the past month. When she finished, she made a copy, then handed one to Voklane. "I hate to admit this, but I don't know if I'll be able to keep my duplicate safe."

Ryan accepted the paper. "All right, thanks. What about the magic lily dust?"

Ciarra sighed. "I don't know, that's so new, we're still learning what's addictive about it, let alone fatal."

"Maybe the new cases will give you insight," he said softly.

"Perhaps. Does the FIO want to be kept apprised?" she asked.

"Not unless you think I need to know something," Ryan answered. "Though I'll be out of the city for a bit. Not sure how long I'll be gone."

He and Terran exchanged some kind of a cryptic,

male look that made Ciarra have to resist rolling her eyes. "I'm not the enemy here, guys."

Ryan's gaze shifted to her. She swore a sheen of white flared in his pale irises. She blinked.

"I know," Voklane said. "We're not keeping secrets."

Ciarra glanced between them. "All right."

Ryan nodded and then left. The clank of metal on metal brought Ciarra's attention back to the exam table. Terran had removed the sheet completely and was in the process of cutting the victims gown free.

"She definitely bit at least one person," he said thoughtfully, manipulating the victims jaw and peering into her mouth. "Do you think you could call the containment facility and see if they have any bite victims as patients?"

"Yes. Can you check the others so I can get an idea of how many they should have, or if we need to send a containment unit on the hunt for anyone hiding in the area?"

He yanked the sheet back over the body. "Sure."

Ciarra waited for him in the corridor while he rewashed his hands. At each room, she checked the information inside the door. Terran checked each syndrome case to see if they'd managed to bite anyone. None of the others had, and Reese, a Medical Science Technician, waiting for his MSI to begin an investigation into a magic lily dust overdose incident, looked up when Ciarra stuck her head into the room.

"Oh, hey Shield Guardianess," he said, laying out surgical instruments on a small metal table. "Going to be a long day."

"Yes, sadly it is," she agreed.

"Did you hear how odd the HRS situations were?"

he asked, glancing up between making sure each silver utensil was perfectly aligned.

She sensed more than saw Terran slide in behind her at the door to listen. "Aside from so many at once?"

Reese shrugged a lanky shoulder. "Yeah, had to be scary. But they all died within minutes of going active."

Terran stepped the rest of the way into the room. "Minutes? Are you sure?"

"Um." Reese blinked, his hand hovering over the table holding a scalpel. "Those were the reports."

Ciarra caught Terran's gaze before he rushed from the room. An uncomfortable knot formed in her stomach. "Did you hear anything else?"

The dark length of hair hanging over his eyes flopped back and forth when he shook his head. "Who was that?"

"Terran Kaine," she answered absently, looking over the paperwork on the victim laying on the table. "He's a MedPath."

Metal clattered. "I didn't think they were real," the young technician whispered.

Ciarra smiled. "He gets that a lot."

She put the documents back and went in search of her mythical husband-to-be, trying to keep the nerves dancing in her belly from showing to anyone she passed.

TERRAN MUTTERED AS HE RUSHED THROUGH HIS notetaking. Notes only he'd be able to touch, taking them hastily in the midst of each exam without decontaminating. By the fifth victim, he'd been too anxious to confirm his suspicions to worry about being clean for a dead body. Now, he sat on a stool, using an extra tool table to write observations while he reached over to have another close look at the virus. He'd managed to do thorough physical exams on each victim, though he hadn't performed any autopsies. The evidence he'd found made him believe one wouldn't be necessary. Not for him.

The death of the current victim was listed as an overdose. Except he'd found the virus when he'd had a hunch to check. The mutated strain was different than the others he'd encountered. Too fragile to live long, which accounted for the mere minutes of frenzied behavior before the victims died. Or in this case, had only become infected long enough to die, when the virus died with them instead of taking over in an effort to spread through bites.

The faint creak of the door opening drew his attention long enough to notice who walked in. Ciarra closed the door and leaned against it, sighing heavily. Terran quickly wrote his thoughts before they deserted him. Even fatigued and overwhelmed, Ciarra was a sight he wanted to indulge in with far greater interest than the one lying cold inches away.

"They have a single bite victim," she announced, pushing off the door. "Sorry it took so long for me to let you know, I've been trying to reach Arch Guardian Eslainte all afternoon to allocate additional MSI's and MSO's to help here and at the containment facility. I'd even take any spare MST's from the hospital that are willing. I don't have enough staff to deal with this influx."

Terran carefully dropped the pen he'd used into the metal can marked *Burn Waste*. He folded the paper and laid it in the center of an open file. "You may not have as big of an issue as you think."

She waited until he'd turned off the water from decontaminating his hands before speaking. "You found something."

He closed the file and then carefully slipped it into a large envelope. He wrote *Do Not Touch* across the front. "I think I know how they were all infected without coming in contact with a host. At least, not a host in the true sense of the word."

Arms crossed, she remained quiet, brows lifted in expectation.

"All the remains brought in today had the virus."

She blinked and paled, her arms falling to her sides. "What?"

"The five supposed overdoses died of HRS, not magic lily dust, but the virus died, too."

"And the ones who became active?"

"I found some powder residue on one victim's upper lip, so I checked the others and found evidence of the lily dust on each of them." He took a deep breath. "I think the virus is somehow being transmitted through the dust to unsuspecting users."

"Whoa." Eyes wide, she held her hands out. "Wait a minute, just... wait. HRS is transmitted sexually, it needs body fluids to survive. How could it be in powder form?"

He raked a hand through his hair. "I don't know. I'm still trying to figure out that aspect. Maybe that's one of the reasons it's too weak to survive long. While fast acting, really fast, it's almost... unhealthy. I don't know how to describe it any other way. Something about the mutation is *wrong*."

"The entire situation is wrong," Ciarra muttered and then took a long breath, though she remained ashen. She swept her hand toward the body. "Do you think we need to autopsy?"

"I wasn't going to, but I think at least one overdose victim should be," he answered after some thought. "But it can wait. I want to take a look at the bite victim, and anyone else processed today at the containment facility."

"The rest?" She opened the door and leaned against it to wait while he walked past.

"You can sign for cremation and release."

"That'll make my MSI's happy to know." Hands shoved deep into her lab coat pockets she fell instep beside him. "Should I radio the Arch Guardian back and cancel my message?"

Terran tapped the envelope with his notes inside. "I'm not sure. If tomorrow is this bad again, you'll need help."

"And a place to store more bodies," she said with a frown. "I'll make sure they send as many to the crematorium today as they can." Then she puffed out a breath and rubbed a finger between her brows. "I hate that we're having this conversation."

He wrapped an arm around her shoulders and pulled her into his side. "I know."

An observation window looked in on two MSI's looking over a body, clipboards in hand. Ciarra slipped away and went into the room. Terran waited while she conveyed instructions. They stopped two more times before heading out of the building to her Ariot.

A chill hung on the edge of the breeze as they stepped outside. Bright green spring leaves danced playfully in the soft currents. Terran tilted his head to the sun and breathed in deep. The stench of death, disease, and drugs filtered away. Ciarra's cool fingers slid between his.

"Are you doing okay?" she asked softly, bumping her hip to his.

He squeezed her hand as they wove between parked Ariots and the occasional bicycle. "Yes, just wish I knew how the virus was being isolated, let alone manipulated and put into something it should be impossible to survive in."

"A lot of questions." She stopped at her Ariot. "Voklane said he was leaving today?"

"Yes, so we're on our own." He shifted until he faced her. "Why?"

Her expression darkened, and she released his hand. "I don't know much about Gen-Heir talents, and with the virus being something so specific, I thought maybe he would know someone we could ask."

Terran rubbed his jaw. "Eslainte may know, since she's the Arch Guardian over Medical Science."

"And a true Medical Scientist talent," Ciarra said, her words thoughtful. "She can only see into the living though, right? Unlike you?"

"I'm not sure how her talent works," Terran admitted. "Living or dead, a body is a body."

"But a Sympath can't touch a corpse and feel the last emotions experienced, so perhaps she's the same. She needs life to be able to peer inside. But maybe she would know of a talent, like a MedPath, only that can work *outside* a person."

The train of the thought left him uneasy. "Would explain a lot, though I hope not."

She nodded. "Me too."

Another swift breeze rushed by, fluttering her jacket and shaping her clothes to her frame. Terran didn't want to think about deadly viruses or impossible situations with equally deadly results. Not when the woman in front of him provided such an exquisite distraction. He slid his hand free from hers and up her arm to her jaw. Leaning in close, he applied pressure until she tilted her head back. His lips brushed hers in soft, fleeting kisses.

"Before we go to the containment facility," he said, rubbing his nose to hers and fluttering his lips across hers again, "let's stop by the records department and sign our contract."

Her breath caught and she leaned back, her gaze searching. A slow smile curled her lips. "All right."

10

MARRIED. THE WORD ROLLED AROUND IN CIARRA'S BRAIN, unfurling emotions she didn't have time to examine. Casting a sideways glimpse at her... *husband*... the strongest she had to shove deep, deep down. Or find a closet and properly reestablish their union. All too vivid memories of their interrupted morning kept replaying in her mind. The firm warmth of muscles she couldn't wait to explore, to learn. Wondering, not for the first time, if all the same places still made him respond, or if she'd discover new ways to make him lose control.

The contract signing had been as uneventful as the first time. Only instead of writing in a decade, Terran had penned in *life*. No going back, she was in their relationship good or bad. A faint tremble danced in her stomach. She still hadn't decided if she missed a promise ceremony or not. If they wanted one in the end, she figured they could have one just the two of them. They were the only ones accountable to the promises they'd make anyway. Her father had been absent, by her choice, in the renewal of her marriage. Not that she

126

had any clue to his whereabouts. This time, he had no place in her relationship, at any stage.

Terran processed a line of potential patients, while she occupied a stool at the exam table. The staff had been overwhelmed when they'd walked into the containment facility. Since the bite victim was confined on the verified floor, Terran had stepped in to help. With a touch, he could send a person home, or up to isolation. So far, they'd all been released. Terran wrote a few notes as the last person left.

"I guess I shouldn't be surprised," Ciarra said, draping her stethoscope around her neck. "But, I am."

"Let's go look at the bite victim." He closed the file and stood.

Ciarra propped her elbow on the table and looked him over. "Are you going to cut your hair?"

The change in subject didn't seem to faze him. He reached over his shoulder and grabbed the end of his ponytail. "I haven't decided."

Smiling, she pushed back from the table and stood. "I like it."

"Then I guess I'll keep it long. For now," he said, taking her hand.

At the stairs, he held the door for her. Ciarra grasped the cold metal rail and glanced over her shoulder. The door closed on a banging echo as he kept pace behind her. She wished she knew what everything they'd discovered so far meant. Not a single positive HRS victim after ten active cases in one morning. The impossibility of the situation almost made her stumble. Terran's hand settled on her hip, steadying her.

She looked over her shoulder at him again. "Thanks."

"Are you okay?"

"I'm just…" She shook her head and let out a frustrated breath. "I'm confused about the virus. And worried."

"Me too," he said, his hand falling away.

The cold he left behind made her frown deepen. At their floor, an attendant cleaning the floor with a mop and disinfectant looked them over. His gaze lingered on Terran's coat. Color faded from his caramel toned face and he teetered, staggering back. The bucket clattered. Water sloshed over the edge and slapped the floor. Terran ignored the dramatic reaction, continuing to walk, peering into each observation room.

Ciarra shook her head and joined their hands, pleased when he accepted the gesture. "How do you tolerate such reactions to you?"

"I'm used to them," he said with a shrug. "People have always been afraid of what they don't understand, and they've never understood me. No human should be able to see something unseeable, let alone be immune to what is fatal to every other person in the inhabited world."

"Except another MedPath."

He bumped his shoulder to hers and smiled. "Of which we are so few we're more a legend than a reality to most."

Ciarra slowed. "What other legends are there about talents?"

A huddled figure behind glass appeared on their right. Terran stopped and unwound their hands. He pressed his fingertips to the glass. The patient looked up, her vivid blue eyes red-rimmed, her short blonde hair knotted. A thick white bandage dotted with blood wrapped around her forearm. She curled deeper into herself and scooted into the corner of the bed.

"I don't know of many legends, just other interesting genetic abilities. Such as being able to connect with an animal, or a plant, or even an inanimate object like a gun."

"What about a virus?" she asked, her mind conjuring a horrible scenario. "Do you think someone could somehow bond with a virus?"

"Is that what you wanted to ask Arch Guardian Eslainte?" he asked, looking down at her. She nodded and he shrugged. "Even if they could, how would they remove it from the host, let alone manipulate it into a mutation?"

"I don't know. But like you said, we don't know how your talent works. What if…" She touched a shaky hand to her upper lip and whispered, "What if someone can do all that? Manipulate a mutation and change how it's able to be transferred?"

Terran inserted his key into the door. "Then we're in *big* trouble."

"It's okay," Terran urged softly when the young, terrified woman flinched away from him again. The sage green hospital gown she wore, unique in color to the containment facility, encompassed her entire body. She'd pulled her legs up under it and wrapped her arms around her knees, effectively hiding in the billowing mass of cotton.

"I'm not going to hurt you," he assured, sitting on the opposite end of the bed from her. "I just want to check on the status of the virus."

"I was bit," she sniffled, burying her face in arms.

"I know, but the virus in the man who bit you, there's something wrong with it. You may not have been infected." He held his hand out. "I want to check, if you'll let me."

"Everyone who is bit is infected," she argued, a tear slipping down her cheek. "I'm going to die, and I won't be responsible for putting anyone else through this."

"A brave thing." he said, motioning with his fingers. "But, perhaps not necessary. Let me see. Just your wrist, that's all I need, I promise."

Hand trembling, she reached out. Terran pressed his fingers into the tender flesh of her inner wrist and closed his eyes. He focused his talent, as he had downstairs, and waited for the images of healthy cells flowing through veins to filter into his mind. Once the connection was made, he began a careful, thorough search for the deadly pathogen.

"You have a cut on your foot, that isn't looking good," he murmured. "A different bacterium is present in the cut on your arm. I don't think they cleaned it well."

She sniffled. "They didn't clean it at all. I'm going to die anyway, remember?"

Anger heated in his chest. "That's no excuse. You should have been cared for."

Then Terran realized, who would ever find out if she wasn't? They slipped food through a hatch at the bottom of the door, and anything else she required. When the virus overtook her and she became active, they'd wait until the event took its course and she collapsed, completely dead, before entering to take care of her, and the mess she would make of the room. If the infection in her arm became too much for her to bear, no one would notice. Her screaming, begging and crying would be attributed to her distress due to the HRS.

Terran concluded his exam. "There is no sign of the virus in you."

"But, I was bitten," she stated again. "I'm *going* to get sick."

"You will get sick if your wound isn't treated, but not from human rabies syndrome."

She stared at him, holding her injured arm to her chest.

Terran stood and made notes. "I'm going to have your wound treated, and then you're free to go."

"No!" Horror filled her wide eyes. She balled tighter into the corner. "No, I'm not going to turn into monster. I'm not going to do this to anyone else."

He touched a hand to the toes peeking out from under her gown. "Stay as long as you need. But you aren't going to become a monster."

She rocked, her arms tightening around her knees. "I won't let it happen, I won't…" she whispered the vow over and over again.

Terran knew he'd lost her. She'd gone to a place only time would help pull her from. The young female patient however, would make history. The first bite victim to survive with the memory of the attack, and live to talk about the event. Perhaps she'd be the only one, if they managed to figure out what was going on.

Outside the room, Terran continued to observe her heartbreaking behavior. Ciarra stepped next to him, arms crossed. Her troubled expression reflected in the glass.

"Is she okay?" she asked.

"She's not infected, and no, she's still not okay. She's suffered the equivalent of a violent assault without the hope of survival most victims have. At least that's the frame of mind she's stuck in. She'll need the same level of support an assault victim receives if she's to make it through this." Terran shifted until his shoulder leaned against the glass. "Did you know your MSO's or technicians aren't treating bite victim wounds?"

"What do you mean?"

"I mean, they wrapped her arm in a bandage and tossed her in this room. No debriding, no pain salve, no antibiotics. Nothing." He forced the rage trying to rise down again. "Why?"

"I imagine fear. The virus is active in the wound," she answered, her hand rubbing her arm, which he noted was covered in goosebumps.

"There is protocol in place for that, to keep whatever Medical Science Officer is providing her care, safe. Fear is no excuse to allow suffering. Already an infection is setting in, and I have to wonder over the past five years how many others were in agony when their time finally arrived." He shook his head in disgust and headed for the staff desk. "We expect people to come here of their own free will, to do the right thing, and then don't even provide them with basic comfort or care? Unacceptable."

"I had no idea," she said, having to almost run to keep pace with him.

Terran slowed his steps and tried to calm the tension bunching his muscles. "Who is currently in the Master Guardian Danellis seat?"

The first person to hold the Master Guardian rank over the Haven City containment facility had been a man named Mitch Danellis, a hundred years ago. The seat would always hold his family name, in his honor. At one time, the position had belonged to Terran. Then he'd married Ciarra, and kept the rank until she would have surpassed him as Shield Guardian Levkaseon, and he'd have taken on her rank in a supportive role. By taking his name, she'd be forced to give up her ranking at the next Endowment and Revocation meeting. Though if they discovered her father's involvement in the HRS epidemic, she'd lose it anyway. Or rather the family would, since ranks could be inherited.

"Nevalyn Sealocke, I don't think you ever met her. She worked at the Port Anchor containment facility before being awarded the Master Guardian position here," Ciarra replied. "She's been great for the facility. Not as good as you, granted. But who could be? I can't imagine she's aware her MSO's aren't caring properly for patients."

Terran ignored the irritation at the reason why another had been brought in to oversee the facility. He'd been shipped off to prison. A situation the current Master Guardian had no control over, or part of. "How do you allow something like that to slip by?"

Ciarra shrugged. "You trust your staff. If they say their floor is doing well, and a walk through confirms, how else would she know? None of the patients complain. They're too upset to do much more than what we just walked away from."

Shaking his head, Terran stopped at the empty station desk. "I guess I ran things a little differently."

Ciarra leaned her elbows against the edge of the counter. "As I said, no one could really replace you."

Terran closed the short distance between them and

brushed a kiss across her lips. "And aren't I thankful for that?"

A soft sigh slid between her lips before she opened under his gentle assault. Her tongue welcomed him in. The sweet flavor of her burst across his senses, enticing and alluring. He pulled back before the hunger sparking to life inside him could grow.

She licked her lips, her eyes dark with desire. "Are you almost finished here?"

Terran ran his thumb along her glossy bottom lip. "After I make sure the bite victim is cared for, yes."

Ciarra grabbed his hand so fast and tugged, he couldn't help but laugh. She froze and stared at him. "That's the first time you've laughed."

Smiling, he touched a finger to her jaw. "I have something to be happy about."

A familiar glow filled her eyes and she opened her mouth to speak. But as desperately as he wanted to hear the words he was certain she was about to utter, he didn't want to hear them in the hall of the containment facility. Not when he couldn't do anything to seal them. Terran kissed her quickly and shook his head. "Wait," he said. "Please wait."

She understood what he asked and nodded, smoothing a strand of hair behind his ear. "Okay, I will."

Still holding his free hand, she led him to the stairs. They went to the top floor, where the lab, Master Guardians office, and administration were located. Like Ciarra, the Master Guardian Danellis was young for her position. However, she listened and was equally frustrated to learn her Medical Science Officers were lax in their treatment. She promised to deal with the situation and ensure they tended to the female patient. Also assuring him the terrified woman could remain as long as necessary to convince her she wasn't a danger to the public.

"I know you explained it to the Master Guardian, but let me make sure I understand," Ciarra said, waiting on the landing while he made sure the top floor was secured. "The virus had time to kill and animate, but not time to make it to the saliva glands to spread?" She shook her head in confusion. "I don't understand. I thought that happened simultaneously."

"Perhaps in the regular strain, it does. I mean, from what I know, we haven't been able to have a MedPath present when the virus hits its active stage to know exactly what's going on. To be able to visually capture that, we'd have to have at least two MedPath's on duty at every moment, with the patient secured to a bed and a MedPath in continuous contact to watch the progression. We're too few to be able to pull off such an experiment.

"Even Ruthenia, the largest population of Gen-Heirs, doesn't have enough of us for a full, uninterrupted study of the virus in action," he explained, motioning for her to head down the stairs. "What we know is based on pre-cataclysm information, visual observation from attacks, and what we've witnessed in containment facilities. The reality could be far different. All I know is with the mutated strain the virus wasn't present in the saliva."

"I'm going to have to write up a report. I have to let Arch Guardian Eslainte know what's happening. I can't wait on her to get back with me. I have no idea how to handle this, or what happens if this new, faster acting strain mutates again, only becomes contagious. We could be looking at another population terminating level event." Anxiety laced her voice and made her steps heavy on the stairs.

Terran let out a heavy breath. "I don't think we need to be thinking about that stage of panic. Not yet. The virus isn't stable. I can promise you that much."

"But mutations happen. I mean, this is one, right?" She glanced at him on the landing before starting down another set.

"Yes, but I already told you, I don't think it's natural."

"Could it mutate to become more stable?"

He considered her question carefully. "I don't believe so. At least, not without the assistance it's already received. Whatever that may be."

Her heavy sigh echoed around the open space. "This is so frustrating. I wish we knew more, or who could even be capable of altering a virus. Either through a talent, or some advanced means they've managed to keep hidden."

"That ma—"

Plaster exploded behind Ciarra's head. A small hole appeared, haloed by broken bits of wall. Ciarra ducked, covering her head and stumbling down the last few steps. Terran grabbed the door to the fourth floor and yanked. He shoved her through. Metal chinked off metal as a bullet hit the railing they'd held onto seconds before. Rows upon rows of patient records and storage boxes lined the entire floor. Windows provided weak lighting when no one worked to light the lamps. The musky scent of old paper filled the open space. Grabbing Ciarra's hand, Terran sprinted across the wide corridor made by the seemingly endless stretch of shelving units.

Adrenaline pounded through his veins, and he had to fight not to stash Ciarra somewhere safe and figure out how to confront whoever shot at them. Knowing they may not be alone, and not wanting to leave her unprotected, kept him focused on getting to safety. They didn't have long before whoever was shooting at them realized where they'd escaped. Terran hoped to be into the other stairwell by then.

"What...?" Ciarra gasped, her hand squeezing his tight.

"I have no idea," Terran answered her half-spoken question, resisting the urge to look over his shoulder, which would only slow them down. "But we can't stay here, we're wide open and easy targets."

"I don't understand," she huffed. "That... was a bullet... right?"

"Yes."

"Oh, summer sun," she breathed out. "That's a bit of a step from burning documents."

"A bit," he agreed and increased their pace until he knew she wouldn't be able to keep up if he went any faster. "Someone definitely wants what we're finding silenced."

Her breathing went from fast to frantic.

"Don't panic on me now, sweetheart," he urged, dragging more than guiding her to the nearing door.

He swung the door open, ducking when a sound at the other end of the floor alerted him they were no longer alone. Wood splintered in the door frame.

"He's not the best shot," Terran said, pulling her to safety and then using his key to lock the door and maybe buy them enough time to get to the ground level, the most populated floor. Of course, there was no guarantee their would-be assassin would avoid shooting into a group.

Ciarra's gray eyes were wild with fear. "Not something to complain about."

They navigated the stairs as quickly as they could without falling. No more bullets pinged off the railing or tore chunks from the walls. Terran began to hope the gunman worked alone after all. On the ground floor, business conducted as usual. The technicians, attendants, and MSO's all seemed oblivious to the chase that had happened several floors above. Ciarra forced him to slow, tugging on his hand until he walked at a normal pace.

A man stepped into the bustle of workers moving along the main corridor. Almost a head taller than everyone around him, he wore all black, with a hat obscuring his hair color. He reached into his jacket pocket and time seemed to slow. Terran stumbled back and reached for the nearest door. The knob didn't budge.

Turning, he grabbed her shoulders. "Get into the room, and lock the door."

"What?" Eyes wide, she gripped his forearms.

"Now!" He shoved her back in the direction they'd come.

A smile curled the man's lips as he removed an envelope.

Urgency laced with fear. Terran backed her into the door while she fumbled a set of keys. "No matter what, keep the door locked. I'll knock when it's safe."

"Terran." She gripped his arm, her gaze pleading.

He kissed her hard. "In. Now."

Not wasting another second, she unlocked the door. He had to trust she'd follow the rest of his instructions. A pink cloud of dust exploded in the air. Terran's stomach dropped. People coughed, gagged and spit. In the haze of confusion, the man wearing black disappeared. The first scream added to the chaos mere seconds later, followed by shouts. Terran charged into the hysteria, wondering not for the first time, why people lost all sense of calm when faced with a threat.

The fine pink powder filtered down, settling in some areas, only to be kicked up in others. Four people convulsed on the ground, their eyes rolling into the back of their heads, spittle flying from their gaping mouths. Death hung thick in the air. A woman gnashed her teeth and spun. Her arms hung at her sides, useless. One of the technicians had better motor function in the active state, gnawing on a sobbing man's arm. Mid-bite, he went limp, pulling his victim to the ground with him.

Terran reached for a young woman rocking on her heels, her gaze vacant as drool flowed from her mouth. Her shoulders jerked in a heavy twitch. He wrapped his fingers around her throat and banded his arm around her waist. The flow of her blood, saturated with the unnatural mutation, emerged in his mind. Fascinated, he watched the microscopic contagion attack her brain, attaching and affecting all the necessary parts to reanimate and spread via a bite. Her teeth snapped on a crack of sound. Only, as he watched, the virus failed in a wave. Without even so much as a final breath, she collapsed in his arms. Gone. For the first time in his career, he hadn't had to remove a threat, the danger had exterminated itself.

Just as quickly as the attacks had begun, they ended.

"No one move!" Terran ordered, gently lowering the deceased woman to the floor.

Hushed murmurs flowed through the cowering crowd. Sniffs and quiet sobs joined the whispers. He surveyed the situation. A fine layer of powder coated a small area and lay in patches in the wide corridor and main reception area. Unless the powder was disturbed again and inhaled or swallowed, no one else would be infected.

Terran thought rapidly. "Are the original decontamination showers still located on this floor?"

An older woman, face streaked with tears raised her hand to get his attention and nodded. "Yes, but the door is locked. We d-don't use it anymore."

"Will the master key work?" he asked.

Tears of helplessness filled her eyes. She shrugged. "I don't know."

He held his hands out in a calming manner. "Okay, it's fine, I'll check. Everyone, please remain calm and don't move."

Terran swiftly walked the corridor, mindful of stray powder. He searched the bank of doors until he found the one he needed. Aging gray paint chipped off the door, but the once important message was still visible in fading yellow. Testing his key, the stiff lock released and he let out a breath of relief. He propped the door open. Cobwebs and dust coated the floor. Frosted floor-to-ceiling windows allowed in enough light not to need lamps during the day. Terran went to three showers with removable heads and turned them on.

A heavy sigh of frustration slumped his shoulders as he prepared to decontaminate and check the survivors for the virus, before and after they showered, and attend wounds. Being chased by a gunman and cleaning up after a purposeful infection event was not exactly how he'd planned to spend his first day married again to Ciarra.

11

CIARRA PULLED UP TO TERRAN'S HOUSE CLOSE TO midnight, she guessed by the height of the moon. Terran had done everything alone until Ciarra had managed to locate some ancient protective gear to put on those willing to assist. Including herself, despite Terran's arguing, threatening, and near begging for her to sequester herself somewhere safe, or even go back to his house without him. He'd done enough, and she wouldn't allow him to do more alone. The Master Guardian of the facility had stepped in to direct the clean-up efforts, while Ciarra attended to those she could, and conducted interviews.

She didn't like what she'd learned.

Slumped uncomfortably in the seat, Terran didn't even stir as the engine whirled softly and then went silent. If she left him like that, not only would he awaken with a sore neck, but probably every other body part would be hurting, too. The moon's light washed over the masculine angles of his face. Even in rest, he was a beautiful specimen of a man. Perhaps especially in rest, with the cares of the day gone at least for now.

Ciarra leaned back and allowed herself to simply look at him. Her man. Her husband. Tears stung her eyes. She couldn't believe he'd given her a second chance. Had allowed her the opportunity to prove she wouldn't mess *them* up again. Then he'd gone and saved her life.

Twice.

Hiding from bad guys and out-running bullets wasn't on her list of acquired skills. Nor was knowing when someone decided to become a mass murderer via releasing a contagion. Up until now her rank and position consisted of making sure autopsies were performed respectfully, hot-spots of HRS incidents were contained, city hospitals were following code, and discovering what she could about an addictive pink powder. She mostly sat behind a desk or conducted site inspections. Danger was not part of her job description.

The lack of motion must have finally registered. Terran stirred, stretched and groaned. His eyes remained closed as he sighed heavily and relaxed back into the seat. "We made it."

"Yep. No one followed us."

"Interesting."

"We needed luck some time, hmm?" she asked, popping her door open.

The thin green hospital gowns she wore fluttered in the cold midnight breeze. Both she and Terran were dressed in the ridiculously exposing attire. At his insistence, every person involved in the event had placed their clothing in a bag to be burned, then they showered, and dressed in the only mass apparel available.

Patient gowns. When they'd all walked out of the containment facility like a green gowned army, Ciarra was thankful no one from *The Havener* or *Haven City Chronicle* had been around to document the ludicrous situation.

She shivered and pulled the one she'd put on backwards to cover her back and butt tighter around herself in a useless gesture. The cotton was far too thin to do much more than capture the cold rather than repel. Not to mention her legs, and feet, were completely bare. Terran climbed out of the car, his frame languid and relaxed. A small canvas bag hung over his shoulder. He arched his back and rolled his shoulders, then walked beside her to the house. After fishing briefly in the tote, he produced keys and let them inside. Inky darkness greeted them.

"You go on up," Terran said, his feet slapping on marble as he headed deeper into the house, leaving her in the foyer at the bottom of the stairs. "I'm going to make some notes real quick while you wash up again."

Adrenaline had long since let her down. Somehow, she'd managed to maintain her professional status at the facility. Then, she'd managed to drive them safely home. All she had left was a thin thread of control slipping through her fingers, fast. Taking a shaky breath, she fisted her hands in the cotton at her thighs.

"Terran." She hadn't meant for the desperation to be in her voice.

He froze. The bag slid from his shoulder to the floor. Before she could draw another breath, he was on her, wrapping her in his arms and holding her close. A tremor raced through his body and she realized he hadn't been going off to be alone to ignore her. He'd been going to get a handle on himself. He wasn't as unaffected as he'd appeared.

Ciarra hugged him close, taking strength while assuring him of her own safety at the same time. She didn't object when he swept her into his arms and carried her upstairs. Or when he turned on the shower, peeling the hospital gowns off her and guided her into the warm spray. Nor did she say a word when he cared for her, washing every inch of her, and himself. While he checked her, one more time, for injuries that had never had the chance to exist because he'd been there to keep her protected. And when his fingers pressed to her inner wrist and concentration stole over his face, she didn't interrupt, knowing he needed to assure himself, yet again, she hadn't been exposed to the mutated strain. She waited patiently for when he realized she stood naked before him.

Safe.

Healthy.

His.

She slid her hands up his wet biceps to his shoulders, pressing her body close. The warmth and texture of him weakened her knees and sent a delicious current of need straight to her core. Leaning close, she whispered his name and pressed a kiss to the tendon in his neck. Her tongue chased a water droplet as she breathed in his scent. He shuddered and hugged her close, burying his face in the crook of her neck. Tender kisses rained along her shoulder. A gentle bite at her throat proved he remembered what had the power to make her lose conscious thought over anything except him.

Desire, born of desperation over the danger they

faced earlier, coupled with five years of separation, burned through her. With a little hop, she climbed his body, and wrapped her legs around his lean waist. The unexpected weight of her made him stumble. Cold tile met her back. She gasped and he took advantage of her open mouth, his tongue sweeping inside. His hands gripped her butt, holding her hostage, while his kiss brought her to new, frenzied heights. Carnal, seductive, as hot as the water sluicing over them, he left her panting, moaning with a need only he could satisfy.

"I wanted..." He licked her jaw and kissed her throat.

She didn't pretend not to know what he was trying to say. He'd wanted civilized. A bed. Romance. Not the feverish, barely controlled coming together they headed for. "We have the rest of our lives, forever," she breathed, dropping her head back as he lifted her and took a nipple into his mouth. She sank her fingers into his wet hair. "Oh... I forgot how good... that feels... Please, Terran."

His hand slipped between them, testing her, sliding over her slick flesh. She didn't think she could be more ready. A hoarse groan vibrated against her breast. She should have been embarrassed by how quickly her body responded to him, but she couldn't muster much more than an eager wiggle of her bottom. Much to her satisfaction, he didn't make her wait any longer. He eased into her, one smooth hip roll at time, inch by maddening inch, until fully seated.

"I love how much you want me," he said in erratic breaths in time with his thrusts. "How much you've always wanted me."

Incapable of coherent speech, the best she managed

was a mangled cry. Terran gripped her thigh and pressed his shoulders to hers, holding her in place. His other hand took possession of her jaw and forced her mouth back to his. The kiss he gave rivaled the pounding of his body into hers. Possessive. Demanding. Taking.

She dug her nails into his shoulders and locked her ankles at the small of his back, holding on tight. A sensation he alone had ever been able to give her built slowly, rising like an incoming tide. Amazing and euphoric, Ciarra embraced the rush of pleasure, yanking her mouth free and screaming. Terran gripped the back of her neck and held her close. He stiffened and let loose a muffled groan against her throat, his hips jerking at his release.

Languid moments passed as they caught their breath. Steam swirled and filled the stall. Gradually he pulled out while kissing her and helping her stand. He turned the water off and grabbed their towels. With more lingering kisses, he wrapped her up.

Ciarra smoothed his wet hair from his face and smiled. "Now can I tell you?"

"Tell me what?" he asked, his lips pressing to hers again.

"That I love you."

He looked away before she could gauge his reaction. The towel covered his face as he left the bathroom, giving her a stunning view of his naked form. The barest light from the moon filtered in, accenting every muscled hollow as he walked away. Slinging the towel around his shoulders, he crouched in front of the pellet stove and went to work. A soft amber glow encompassed the bedroom.

Ciarra swallowed against the dryness stuck in her throat. Uncertainty made her move silently to her bag of clothing. While he hadn't rejected her declaration, he hadn't accepted it either. Perhaps she expected too much too soon. Maybe the anticipation she'd seen in him earlier at the containment facility when she'd almost told him had been something else. Not even a full day had passed since he'd decided to forgive. To give her another chance. But wasn't love part of that deal? At least, it was for her. Love, however, couldn't be forced. And five years, and a lot of hurt, stood between them. Since denying her heart wasn't an option, Ciarra didn't regret letting her feelings be known.

"I do you know," she said quietly, pulling on a loose-long sleeved shirt. "Love you."

TERRAN'S HAND FROZE AS HE FED PELLETS INTO THE burgeoning fire. Yes, he knew the affection she claimed was real. If he were honest, the precious gift of her love had begun to mend his shattered heart. But he wasn't yet ready to acknowledge much more than he already had.

Time, thankfully, was on his side. He had the rest of their lives to explore the daily choice of love. To bask in the wonder of their restored marriage. The continued forged path of their lives laid one brick at a time. However, old wounds were still open, reminding him not so long ago, love hadn't been enough. On a controlled inhale, he forced the toxic thoughts away. He couldn't afford to allow the taint of doubt to creep in and unravel the fragile threads they'd begun to weave between them.

"Yes, I know," he replied softly, closing the stove and rising. He pulled the towel from his shoulders and finished drying. "And I'm thankful."

She nodded and released a long breath. Without another word, she disappeared under the blankets. Terran hung both their towels up and then slipped on thin cotton sleep pants. He crawled into bed and gathered her curled form to his body. Burying his face in the drying softness of her hair, he breathed deep. His heart clenched and he held her tight.

"Do you really think we can do this?" she whispered into the darkness, her hands gripping his arms banded around her chest and waist.

"Little late to be asking that question, don't you think?" He nuzzled her neck and pressed a kiss to her shoulder.

She laughed, a sweet sound that had him squeezing his eyes shut, not having realized how much he'd missed hearing her happy. "I know we can do *us*. We have many, *many* years to get it right again. I meant do you really think we can stop what's happening in the city?"

"I hope so," he said honestly. "I wish I knew what they were hoping to accomplish, whoever is behind this."

"You think it's bigger than my father?"

He rubbed his hand up and down her side. "Has to be. This is too big for one person, or even two. There has to be funding somewhere. A money trail for the research alone."

She turned in his arms and propped herself up on her elbow, her head resting on her hand. "I interviewed some of the survivors before they left. One of them mentioned seeing a woman wearing glasses outside the front doors taking notes while the event happened."

Terran sat up and stared down at her. "She was observing. Like a lab experiment."

"To what purpose? What could she have possibly hoped to discover?"

Adjusting pillows at his back, Terran let his weight fall against the headboard, his mind spinning with scenarios. "Think about it. They've been doing small trial runs the past month, but the results haven't been what they wanted, so they did a large run this time." He stopped and quickly corrected himself, "I mean yesterday, morning."

"Only those didn't seem to work out so well either," she mused, joining him up against the headboard.

"Right, and if they conducted them all around the city, they could only observe so many."

"But why execute another test in such a short time? They haven't done that yet if what you're saying is true, they've waited days."

"Or maybe this was their plan all along. After all, they had a bite victim taken there."

Ciarra blinked and clutched at the blankets. Color drained from her face. "And had you not been there, no one would have known otherwise. They could have staged the whole thing to look like some rapid HRS event. Could have given her the powder and made it look like she'd somehow escaped. Do you think that's why we were chased?"

"Maybe." He raked his fingers through his damp hair and leaned his head back, staring up at the shadow-laden ceiling. "There could be any number of reasons for that. To keep us from witnessing, to making sure we were found dead, too."

A dejected sigh left her. "Wow, Terran. This is… so much bigger than I ever imagined."

He wrapped an arm around her shoulder and pulled her into his side. "We'll figure it out. Somehow."

She shifted at his side, and before he could realize her intent, she straddled him. Her fingers slipped into his hair as she laid her torso across his. "We're in bed."

Terran smiled, his hands cupping her butt, thankful for the shift in focus. "Very perceptive of you."

"I don't want to talk about what happened anymore," she said, her breath fanning across his bare chest.

"You started the conversation," he reminded her.

She rose up, capturing his mouth in a hot, wet, open-mouthed kiss. "I did. So, I guess I'm ending it. You were complaining earlier, I figured maybe since I had my way in the shower, you could have yours in bed."

Heated desire surged through him. He rolled them until his hips rested between her parted legs. "Oh really?" he growled, sliding her shirt up to expose her silky skin to his mouth.

She made quick work of pulling her shirt off, while using her feet to force his loose pants off his hips. "We have a lot of time to make up for." Her tongue licked his shoulder up to his ear. "I have missed you. So much."

The tremble in her words mirrored the faint tremor of her body, betraying more than mere lust motivated her. Terran laid his cheek on the pillow of her breasts and listened to her heart beat a strong, steady rhythm.

The heart she'd held out to him and trusted him to care for.

"I don't think more than I could have missed you," he admitted softly.

"Terran," she whispered on a choked sob, wrapping her entire body around him.

"Shh," he urged and rained kisses on her chest, her throat, jaw and to her mouth. The salt of her tears brought an ache to his chest. "The past, Ciarra, it's all behind us. No more of this. No more."

Then he made them both forget about broken hearts and broken promises. He spent the rest of the night showing her all the ways he'd missed her, and all the way's he planned to spend the rest of his life loving her.

12

———————

"Can you get me into Byron's lab?" Terran asked, looking up from the notes he'd been taking.

Ciarra took a bite of fruit and chewed thoughtfully. Bright morning sun streamed in through the lab windows, reflecting off the too big dove-gray button shirt she wore. Her hair was a mess around her head, knotted and sticking up at odd places from their passionate night and having fallen asleep with it still wet. She was utterly sexy. And when she shifted on the table across from him, giving him the barest glimpse to remind him she was naked underneath that shirt, she knew how crazy she drove him.

He took a bracing breath and returned to his notes, trying to recall everything he'd witnessed at the facility the evening before. The temptress feet from him made the task near impossible. "I think," he said, forcing his thoughts back to the important job set before them. "If I can get into his lab, I can figure out what he's been up to. At least, I hope so."

"Unless he isn't the one doing all this," she said,

153

popping another slice of orange into her mouth. "But yes. I think I can get you into his lab. He still works out of the basement in the Shield Guardian house."

"He didn't give that space to you?"

She shook her head and sighed, her attention shifting to the food in her hand. "No. I kept the library as my space. I didn't even get the main suite for my bedroom when I received my rank."

"He kept his status in the house, but not outside of it, is that what you're telling me?" he asked, unable to keep the anger from his voice.

"It's not a big deal," she said on a shrug. "I didn't care."

Terran stood, bracing his hands on the smooth wood table. "You should. When you were approved to take over the Levkaseon Shield Guardian seat, the house associated with the rank became yours. That lab is yours. Everything under that roof not purchased by your father's working funds, became yours. You aren't just a Shield Guardian when you step outside, Ciarra."

She lifted her beautiful eyes to meet his. "The fight didn't seem worth it. Not for rooms in a house."

"It wasn't about rooms for him. It was about refusing to hand over authority. He did it in the eye of the public, but clearly he still sees himself as Levkaseon."

She rolled her eyes and gave a scoffing laugh. "Oh come on, it's a house. My father didn't walk around demanding everyone still call him Shield Guardian."

Terran held her gaze for a quiet moment. "Did he ever recognize *you* as Shield Guardian, or just tell you how to behave?"

"He's not doing my job," she said, her jaw set.

"He didn't have to." Terran sighed and dropped his head. "In fact, not having to worry about the obligation of watching over Haven City Health Services, but still maintaining his power level in whatever he's involved in, probably helped. He kept all the respect and none of the responsibility."

A heavy frown darkened her face. "That's an awful lot to assume based on him keeping rooms in a house."

Terran crossed the short distance between them. He slid his hands up her bare thighs and touched his forehead to hers. "I hope I'm wrong. But a transition of power is just that. A transition. The only thing he transitioned from was an office in a building. Am I wrong?"

By the thinning of her lips and the way she averted his stare, he knew he'd hit a nerve. He pressed a knuckle under her chin and made her meet his gaze. "Am I?" he asked again.

"No," she said with a tremble.

"If that's the case," he said slowly, musing, "then we have to assume he still holds power, still has connections in high places he may be using."

"Wouldn't he still have those as the dowager?"

"Yes and no." He tilted his head back and stared up at the vivid light casting interesting shadows on the high ceiling and considered what to say. How to explain. Under his fingertips, the softness of Ciarra's thighs reminded him they were partners. True partners. In everything.

If they had a chance of getting through this, of discovering even a snippet of the truth, they were going to have to do so together. He couldn't afford to keep anything from her. Nor did he want to. "If he's managed to keep the right people convinced he still holds most, if not all, of the power as Levkaseon, he's likely managed to maintain some level of funding from them as we were talking about this morning, along with some leeway as far as looking another direction when he does things."

"Unless they've ordered those *things*," she said tightly.

"Right. And if they ordered, and he obeyed, it's because he had something to gain from their instruction."

"Not if he was coerced," she argued, forcing his attention back to her.

Terran hesitated. "Ciarra…"

She shook her head and grasped his jaw. "I know you want to think the worst of him. I do. But I just…I can't."

The well of anger took him by surprise. *No.* No, he was supposed to be past this. Beyond the reach of crushing hurt and the sharp wound of betrayal. Taking a deep breath, he stepped away. Hands fisted, he went to the wall of windows and looked out over the low fog-covered fields, to the dark line of trees beyond.

"Trust goes both ways," he said, unable to stop the dangerous bite to his words. "I can't give it unless I'm getting it, too. You have to trust me when I say your father is involved in something bad."

The whisper of her feet on tile sounded behind him. Her hands brushed his hips and wrapped around his stomach. The weight of her body settled against his back. "I do trust you, or I wouldn't have contracted with you. I promise, Terran. But I don't think I can believe he's *all* bad. Not yet. Not without more proof."

He wanted to ask how much more damn proof did

she need? Because she hadn't needed near enough to accept *his* guilt when he'd been sent to rot in prison by her scab of a parent. That path however, led to a new chapter on another shattered marriage. He couldn't afford to go there. Couldn't allow the forgiveness he'd declared to be forsaken.

Steeling his emotions, he separated, assessed and collected his thoughts. They'd been married all of six months when Byron had destroyed the fragile ties they'd forged in a blossoming relationship. Less than a week back into her life, Terran had shattered her safe world for the second time in her adult life. He blamed Byron for both instances. This time, she wouldn't be alone when the full extent of her father's black heart revealed itself. Terran would be there, to help her pick up the pieces.

"I know what you're standing there thinking," she whispered. "I believed him, but I didn't believe you. If my father is truly behind all this awfulness, I'm going to have to accept that. But the bottom line is, I accepted things that were downright inconsequential in the end about you when placed side by side with the crimes we're believing Byron has committed."

He stiffened.

A soft chuckle preceded her nuzzling her his shirt. "See? I knew it. We may have been apart for five years due to my colossal mistake, but I *know* you, Terran Kaine."

Her grip loosened when he turned. Tears brimmed in her eyes. Terran's heart constricted. He cupped her jaw and pressed a tender kiss to her lips.

She gripped the front of his shirt and lifted onto her toes. "And I also know you could have said some really awful, *awful* things to me just now," she murmured against his lips. "Yet, you didn't."

"The past needs to stay there. We can't start over if I can't see you as the woman I love and the future we can have. I don't want to hurt you. I don't want to see you upset. We both seem to be struggling here, and I'm sorry," he replied, echoing her words.

She smiled, a tear sliding down her cheek. "You love me?"

He pressed another soft, lingering kiss to her lips. "I wouldn't have contracted with you if I didn't."

Joy brightened her eyes as more tears welled in them. "We'll get it right this time."

He swiped the tear away with his thumb. "You really need to stop crying on me, woman."

Laughing, she dropped her head to his chest. "I know I do. Perhaps when things aren't so emotional, I might be able to. No promises on that one, though."

Terran buried his hands into the thick weight of her hair and tugged gently until she lifted her head and met his stare. "I love you."

Her chin quivered and another tear splashed onto his hand. "You're not helping stop the waterworks here."

He kissed her again in a slow, sensual play of everything he felt. His tongue swept in unhurried caresses in and out of her mouth. The salt of her tears mingled with the undercurrent of his need. He didn't rush, didn't push for anything else. Still, when he lifted his head, they were both breathless and burning for more.

"When do we have to leave?" she asked, her eyes glazed and half-closed.

"Soon."

She blinked and licked her lips. "Soon, soon?"

He smiled and kissed her again. Longer. Deeper. Until she pressed into the arousal he couldn't deny. "We'll make time."

"Oh, thank you." She exhaled and then wrapped herself around him, reminding him she hadn't bothered to put more than his shirt on this morning.

13

Nervous dread settled deep in Ciarra's stomach. She pressed a firm hand to her abdomen and cleared the rise of bile from her throat. Below the manor, two-thousand square feet of her father's lab stretched out. A locked door, for which she had the key clenched in her hand, waited for them at the bottom of a steep, narrow set of stairs.

Terran waited patiently behind her, a steadying hand on her hip. A reminder she wasn't alone. She knew the passion he'd given into earlier this morning had been for her benefit. The hot and gloriously pleasurable reprieve had taken her mind off the awful things to come. Leaving their bed had taken serious effort on her part. She'd wanted to curl under the covers, delight in the soreness of her body from joining with his and ignore responsibility. A recent recurring theme in her life she couldn't afford to give into.

At the bottom of the stairs, she reached for the door and paused. Garbled voices filtered through the wood. Frowning, she carefully tried the knob. The cool metal turned in her palm, unlocked. Terran squeezed her shoulder, a silent message not to reveal their presence. Ciarra pressed her fingers to the door, allowing it to open enough for a sliver of light to fall on the stairwell. Terran stepped down to join her on the small landing, his shoulder barely touching the whitewashed wood.

Ciarra strained to hear, recognizing her father's voice. Surprised, she blinked and glanced up at Terran. Her father was home, seemingly safe. However, she knew he never rose from bed so early, and if he did, he broke his fast and waited for his morning cough to settle before venturing to any work-related task. As if on cue, he erupted into a violent fit of hacking. She tensed, resisting the habitual urge to ask if he was okay. Terran's hand settled on her hip, calming her tangled nerves.

Bits of conversation floated through the small opening.

"… she?" an unfamiliar voice asked. She couldn't tell whether it was male or female, but the tone spoke of authority.

"I don't know," Byron wheezed.

"… lose …daughter?"

Another nasty cough assailed her father. "I didn't…" He gasped. "Lose her. She's with…"

"You … taken care of … the chance… gave you … means."

"I didn't think he'd ever be a problem again." Her father must have stood closer to the door, for Ciarra didn't mistake or lose any of his words.

The person asked a question too low to be heard.

"He won't be. I talked her out of them before, I can

do so again. She's obedient to me. You know this, you've seen it."

Terran's grip tightened on her waist as Ciarra's muscles stiffened. *Oh no he wouldn't.*

"… a problem… ruin everything."

"No, no, he won't be," her father insisted around another cough. "I'll make sure of it this time."

Again, the stranger's words garbled.

"He knows nothing, and even if he does, we've destroyed all the evidence. He has no proof, just like last time. I haven't failed, you'll see. Just let me talk to her."

Dread and betrayal cut a jagged line to her heart. *Like last time.* After everything Terran had told her, there was no mistaking what those words meant. Ciarra clenched her hands to keep from bursting into the lab and making demands of truth on Byron. She strained to hear more.

"… doesn't talk …failures."

"I'm not a failure," Byron replied, anger thick in his voice. "Everything will go as planned. Ciarra will see the benefit of following the plan. She'll understand it's all for the best."

"…if she doesn't? …. we'll have to do."

"I'll make sure of it, I swear…"

A commotion sounded upstairs. Ciarra sucked in a breath and stared at Terran in panic. They couldn't be caught spying. He made a rapid upward motion, and together, as quietly as possible, they ran back up to the first floor. Two men, one around her age, the other starting to gray, dressed in slacks, white button shirts and black jackets stood in the foyer, arguing with a male staff member.

The younger one, tall and dark haired, spotted her and relief crossed over his face. "Shield Guardianess Levkaseon."

"Can I help you?" she asked, forcing her face into something more welcoming and in charge. Though inside everything trembled and rebelled. Her father was indeed a traitor.

He held his hand out and edged past the domineering member of her household staff. "Justin Beirngrave, I'm the assistant to Shield Guardian Taerraine. This is Scotland Nellekin, he's on staff."

Ciarra chanced a glance at Terran. His expression revealed nothing. She released Justin's hand. The assistant to the head of security for the royal family stood in her house. She tried not to think about the implications. "What can I do for you?"

Justin held his hand out and Scotland produced a file. "We received your request to file a grievance against Arch Guardianess Eslainte."

"Come again?" she asked, leaning closer, thinking she must have misheard.

Clearing his throat, Justin opened the folder. "Two days ago, you filed a complaint that the Arch Guardianess over Sziverian Medical Science has failed to properly address the health crisis in the city. Do you deny such claims?"

Two days ago, Ciarra had left a request for assistance with the Arch Guardianess. Eslainte had failed to reply, but Ciarra hadn't told anyone, except Terran. In the chaos her life had become, she couldn't remember if they'd spoken about her attempts to contact the higher authority. "May I see, please?"

Justin slid a paper free and held it out to her. He pointed at the bottom. "Your name."

The grievance was professionally typed. At the bottom of the paper was indeed her signature. Or at least, a very close match. Heat suffused her cheeks. "I didn't sign, or submit this."

He accepted the complaint back with a speculative look. "Interesting."

"She doesn't know what she's talking about!" her father's strained voice shouted behind her. "The city has been steeped in madness, that..." He waved his pale, wrinkled hand. "Issue needs to be addressed."

Ciarra kept her breathing even when all she wanted to do was submit to the anxiety threatening to consume her. She ignored her father and met Justin's gaze. "The only document I signed of any importance two days ago was the one contracting me to Terran Kaine in marriage."

"You did not!" Byron's nails dug into the tender flesh of her inner arm as he forced her to turn and face him.

Ciarra straightened, nearly the dowager's height in his hunched over state. "For life. And I took his name." She leaned in close, so only he could hear. Her body shook and tears burned her eyes. "I know what you did. What you've done. No more. It's over. You've lost."

His face turned an alarming shade of purple. Spittle flew from his thin lips. A racking cough jarred his thin shoulders. The hold on her arm tightened until his nails felt as though they drew blood. "You... stupid... girl!"

Terran pulled her from Byron's grasp, pushing her closer to the security men. "The only foolish one standing here, Jonatis, is you." He turned to the men. "I think you need to call in the Sziverian National Investigative Division and take a good hard look at the lab downstairs."

Byron spun around, his eyes wild, frantic, his breathing erratic. Ciarra looked, expecting to find the stranger he'd been talking to downstairs. But there was no one. "No," he whispered and then fisted his hands and shrieked. "*No!*"

Terran laced his fingers between hers. "Looks like you're all alone. Hope there's enough evidence you don't take the fall singlehandedly."

When her father attempted to bolt, not that Ciarra figured he would have made it far, Terran intercepted him, wrapping his arm around her father's feeble shoulders. "I don't think so." Terran motioned with his head toward the basement stairs. "Ciarra, why don't you show the gentlemen downstairs and make sure it's secure for someone to radio." He looked back at her father. "This is after all *your house* and I don't think they'll need any further authorization to search the premises."

Ciarra sniffled and blinked away the tears. "No," she agreed. "They won't."

She went downstairs only long enough to ensure they had access to the exterior doors, making it easier for the group Justin had called in to do their job without having to cram up and down the narrow stairs. Once in the lab, she discovered she didn't want to know all her father had done. All he'd conspired to do. All the damage he'd already rendered.

Back upstairs, the silence shocked her. She expected fighting between her father and Terran. But she found them sitting in silence, disturbed only by coughing. She plopped down in a chair across from Byron's hunched and frail form at the breakfast table. Terran rose, giving them the illusion of privacy by going to the kitchen and preparing some food. Not that Ciarra figured she could eat, but clearly he felt the need to take care of her, or at least do *something*. She understood.

"Why?" she asked, not surprised when her voice cracked. She held her hand open across the table when he didn't answer, didn't even look at her. "Why?"

If possible, Byron shrunk more into himself, appearing hollow and weak. He whined something unintelligible underneath a papery, deep-chested cough.

Ciarra fell back in her chair. Dejection washed through her. "You ruined my marriage. You sent an innocent man to prison." She shook her head and looked away from him. "You killed dozens of innocent people. For what?"

Another incoherent mutter and hand wave met her question. He stared blankly at the table, swaying.

Terran gently set a plate of sliced fruit and cheese on the table in front of her. He brushed hair aside from her forehead and kissed her temple. "I think," he whispered, his hand stroking across her back to settle on her shoulder, "that when he turned around and found he'd been deserted, something… broke in him. I couldn't get him to talk, either. Or even look at me."

Ciarra grasped his hand, lacing their fingers together, her eyes fixed on her pale father. Byron didn't seem to have any awareness of their presence. "Whatever plans he set in motion, he probably hoped they'd see something extravagant before his death. A final legacy, if you will."

"A legacy of devastation?" Terran asked.

Ciarra's chest tightened at Byron's continued odd mumbling. At the truth of her husband's statement. "I doubt we'll ever know."

"SNID will find something, that's their job."

Time passed by with little awareness for Ciarra. She tried everything to get her father to say something intelligible. Eventually, she stopped trying as he sat with a vacant stare, his body moving back and forth like an invisible breeze tugged on him. Terran remained behind her, his fingers sliding along the exposed skin of her neck, down her shoulders, her spine and back up. A constant reassuring presence. She poked at the food he'd brought her, nibbling when he insisted or took a bite himself.

The echo of boots on tile made Ciarra look at the entry to the kitchen. A tall, handsome man strode in. His hair, so dark she couldn't determine the color, was pulled back behind his neck. Skin the color of tea with a hint of milk was even warmer in the now setting sun. The serious, almost troubled expression on his face made Ciarra's shoulders stiffen. He wore the typical clothing of a SNID Guardian. Gray slacks, paler gray shirt, and the black jacket with bold white letters stating who he worked for along with his rank. On the back, SNID, along with his rank and position, would be visible to anyone questioning his authority.

He paused, took in the scene, and then continued until he stood close enough to be heard, but not so close as to make anyone uncomfortable. "Shield Guardianess Levkaseon." He held his free hand out, the other holding a thick, leather bound journal. "I'm Guardian Darius Ralston. I'm an investigator and profiler for

Sziverian National Investigative Division. I'll be handling the proof of guilt for your father's case."

Proof of guilt. The words held a finality. Ciarra closed her eyes and nodded. When she felt centered again, she opened them and met the Guardian's peculiar teal eyes and accepted his hand. "I'm not sure how competent he'll be found for any accusation hearing, but my home is completely open to any required search."

Darius glanced at Terran. "I understand you recently contracted."

"Yes," Terran answered.

"Will we have access to that premise as well, if you don't reside here?"

"If necessary. But Jonatis never set foot there. I've been living at the address for a little over a week," Terran said. "Ciarra has only stayed with me two nights."

Pen scratched on paper and Ciarra resisted the urge to fidget. She'd never been on this end of the process before. "We may have some relevant information at the house, though, as we've been investigating the HRS incidents that seem to be in conjunction with magic lily dust."

"Yes," Darius said, a bit distractedly. "There was plenty of evidence of magic lily dust in the lab. We're having to proceed very cautiously."

"I can help," Terran said. When Darius glanced up, he added, "I'm a MedPath."

"Ah, perfect. They will really appreciate that."

Terran chuckled, but the action was anything but warm. "Yeah, I'm sure they'll appreciate not having to worry about turning into a zombie. I know I will be thankful no one else has to die."

Darius sighed. "Indeed." His attention shifted to her father. "I'd say I'll send for someone from Health Services to evaluate him, but you're the Shield Guardian. Can I trust you to make an accurate assessment?"

"Yes," she stated quietly. She cleared her throat and tried again. "Yes. I believe he should be taken to a mental facility for further evaluation. I know there are two in the city with prison level security."

"He may have to remain there," Darius said slowly. "Even if he's found guilty."

"I understand." And really, what better place? A sane person did not conspire to mass murder. "You aren't put off by Terran's talent?"

Darius shook his head, a smile toyed at his lips. "No." He used his pen to point at his chest. "Beast Master family. One of my younger brother's is the Arch Guardian Wolvengard. We know all about genetic abilities that make people fidget."

Darius asked a few more questions and then waited with them for someone to come and collect her father. When the last Guardian left the property, setting up a time in the morning for Terran to arrive and safely collect evidence and clear the lab of any contagions, Ciarra finally gave in to tears. Again.

14

---

2 Months Later
Haven City, Sziveria
Endowment and Revocation

"Well?"

Terran smiled at the Ciarra's question, so much emotion packed into such a small word. Anxiety pinched her face and showed in the way she bounced in anticipation. He pulled the endowment record out from behind his back. She squealed and reached for the thick sheet of paper with pressed ink. She brushed her fingers over the Sziverian insignia, underneath LEVKASEON - Shield Guardian Rank- Assigned to the KAINE Family, was printed. The sense of pride felt... odd. Yet, he experienced it all the same.

She let out a deep breath. "This is amazing."

Terran wrapped his arm around her shoulders and urged her to walk, guiding her steps. "Only amazing thing about it is they actually gave a Shield Guardian rank to a former convict."

"You're doing it again," she groused, forcing him to stop when she did.

Terran glanced down at the official document still clutched firmly in both her hands. "Doing what again, love?"

"Devaluing yourself. Don't do that." She held the paper out to him. "They cleared your record, or you wouldn't have been able to earn this."

He pulled her tighter into his side, accepting the document. The tattoo forever branded into his skin flashed. "Cleared or not, I'll always have the memory and I will always carry the mark that will make me have to explain, or ignore, people's curiosity."

She wrapped a hand around his wrist draped over her shoulder. "I say ignore."

"Are you sure you're okay with this?" he asked, not for the first time since the rank had been revoked from her.

"I'm still Guardianess Levkaseon, just in a supportive role instead of main. And yes, for the hundredth time, I'm fine. I get to be part of the team again instead of leading it. I'm excited. And we both know I'm really lucky. They could have denied me any Guardian role, and you as well." She nudged his side. "So, do we get to keep the house or are we back in the old ranked property?"

He grinned. "We get to keep our house."

"Good," she said on an exhale. "I never want to go back to the other house again."

He headed to the exit, still keeping her tucked in close. The crisp floral scent of her made him breathe deep. He'd never have to go a day without taking her in. Warm afternoon sun greeted them outside. Terran took a moment to appreciate the beautiful day and the woman at his side. "Are you ready for your father's accusation hearing?"

"It's just a formality at this point. Thanks to Guardian Ralston, my father's involvement in the HRS epidemic is widely documented. The Jonatis name will not be associated with all the good he did in his career, but rather the horror he inflicted on a city." She pressed in tighter to him and Terran hugged her close. "I wish for so many things to have been different."

"I do, too," he admitted. "I also wish we knew *how* they'd been able to manipulate the virus and change its method of infection. Hopefully whoever helped him stays gone."

At the Ariot, she pulled away. "At least we know why. I can't believe he really thought creating an emergency situation behind the Arch Guardian's back would allow him to remove her from power and place me in it."

"He's in the mental hospital for a reason," Terran reminded her.

She sighed, sadness darkening her gaze. "I know, it's just... so many people died for a power play. I'm still struggling with my father doing such an awful thing. And now he's back to being incoherent, so we'll never learn who helped him. Do you think he's faking it?"

"I think," Terran said carefully, meeting her gaze over the top of the vehicle. "The only reason he's still alive is because he has nothing useful to say anymore. Him being delirious has probably saved his life."

"I know, I've considered that as well," she said,

rubbing her forehead. The sun glittered off the paler strands of blonde in her hair.

Terran rapped his knuckles on the thin metal roof. "Ryan Voklane knows, too. So does Darius Ralston, and Justin Beirngrave. We have to trust they'll know what to do with the information. We have Health Services to run, let them worry about what we can't."

She lifted her hands in the air and let loose a long exhale. "You're right. You are absolutely right. Not our place, not our concern anymore."

Terran offered her a gentle smile. "It's okay to want to know who dragged your father through the mud, Ciarra."

"We both know he wasn't dragged. He tromped right on through without any help, getting dirtier and dirtier." She growled and yanked her door open. "I just don't know who they'll go after next. If they could get to a Shield Guardian..."

Holding up the assignment record, he said, "They aren't going to get to *this* Shield Guardian."

"No," she said, her eyes bright with determination. There was his beautiful wife. "They aren't."

THANK YOU FOR READING!

WINTERSFALL
Continue reading for an excerpt

CHAPTER ONE

Sziveria, June 7th, 832 P.C.E. (Post-Cataclysm Event)
   Old Helston locality

Chaos erupted in the wake of a bullet piercing a target secured to a giant oak tree. Birds squawked, taking flight in a mass exodus of feathers and trembling leaves. The satisfaction of another perfect shot failed to ease the fiery pain in Katria Nachemir's side from the rifle's recoil. A side effect of not being healed enough to practice.

The exercise provided a much-needed distraction, but the ache brought a reminder of the devastation she attempted to escape. Tears burned her eyes, and with a quick breath, she pushed on, loading two more bullets into the bolt action chamber.

Shooting at a target wouldn't change anything. Her mother and sister were still dead, buried in what would now become a family cemetery. A bullet wound would forever mar her body. Escaping was nothing more than a mental game now. Anytime she looked down at herself, the nightmare would be made real again.

The gunman who stole their lives remained elusive, the reason for the fatal attack unknown. Focusing her pain on something productive was all Katria could think to do. Sitting in the too-quiet house with her despairing father wasn't an option anymore. At some point, perhaps hours after the massacre, he'd forgotten he had one daughter left alive. Katria couldn't take being ignored any longer.

The target became the manifestation of her pain, and the bullet a means to end it. Taking a long, slow inhale, she wrapped her hands around the gun. Her fingertips formed a connection with the rifle. All the working mechanisms became a map in her mind, while the wind blowing across her skin became an adversary. Without effort on her part, the calculations flowed through her.

Before she could pull the trigger again, a twig snapped behind her. She swung around and took aim on the stranger before he moved another step. His hands flew into air. Strong morning light cast his face in sharp relief, drawing attention to a firm jaw, high cheekbones, a patrician nose and a mouth that didn't look to smile often.

"I'm just here to talk," he stated in a deep, soothing voice, his foot lifted midstride. "My name is Ryan Voklane, I work with the First Intelligence Office."

Katria didn't lower the weapon or allow her surprise to show. The FIO Guardian was a long way from home. "Are you here about my mother and sister?"

He slowly removed a tan ivy cap he'd been wearing, revealing neatly combed pale blond hair. He lowered his foot and sank into a non-threatening, relaxed stance. "No, local enforcement is handling that, I believe."

Anger flared. Somehow, Katria managed to keep her temper in check. "And getting nowhere. It wasn't a local murder."

"I'm sure you're aware of your father's past. They may never find who killed them," he said gently.

Fresh tears burned, and she looked away from the pity in his silvery blue eyes. "Then what do you want to talk about?"

"You."

That brought her attention back. "Me?"

"Yes. Do you mind lowering your gun?"

Katria looked him over. Though broad-shouldered and fit, his neatly pressed black pants and jacket, well-tailored gray vest and red silk scarf spoke of days spent in an office. There were no telltale bulges of a hidden gun or knife, at least from his front. If he opted to pull something from his back, she'd be quicker. She decided he likely wasn't much of a threat and lowered her gun. "You're from Haven City?"

"Correct."

"Am I in trouble?"

"No, I'm here to offer you job. A position on one of our elite Guardian teams."

Katria kept her surprise internal. "A position? As what?"

"Sharpshooter."

She glanced down at the worn rifle in her hands. "There's nothing special about my shot."

"On the contrary, Miss Nachemir. You may be the best shooter in Sziveria. Perhaps even the world. You're a Gen-Heir."

Katria kept her expression carefully neutral. Inside, she panicked. She couldn't have been more stunned if he'd slapped her. Yes, she was her father's genetic heir, or Gen-Heir as society preferred to call those who inherited more than looks and health. Her unique capability to connect on a cellular level with a gun, and the knowing by touch alone, of how all its variables—distance, wind, humidity, air temperature and density—affected a shot. With only a rifle, scope and target, her mind calculated and adjusted in a split second. Despite Aleksandrov Nachemir's best efforts, someone had learned the assassin's daughter shared his talent.

"How could you possibly know that?" she asked. "I've never competed, never done anything outside this property with my father."

"We have our ways."

She frowned. "Of course you do."

"I know this is a delicate time for you, but if you work with us, I promise I'll put the full resources of the Sziverian National Investigative Division into the death of your mother and sister. We'll find who killed them, bring them to justice." He took a tentative step forward, his cap clutched in his hands. "Your country needs the skills you have to offer, and you'll be working with the best."

A tightness formed in her chest. *Justice.* A month ago, the word hadn't had much meaning. Now it meant everything. But at what cost? She looked down the length of field to the target on the thick tree trunk. "I'll be doing what someone did to us... won't I?"

"No, no, you'll never take an innocent life. Our Queen Elect has no desire for personal vendettas. She's interested in national security only. When you're called to work, you can be assured the person will be a bad person. Someone like the man who came after your family. Justice *for* another family, for your country."

The words were careful in their assurance. Pretty in their seduction to compel her agreement. Katria looked him over again. The handsome planes of his face remained unthreatening, open, almost warm. She *wanted* to say yes. "My father will never agree."

"You're eighteen, and if I'm correct, uncontracted for marriage?"

"Yes, correct."

The Guardian took another brazen step closer. "You wouldn't have to tell him."

Lie to her father? The idea made acid curl in her stomach, and yet the suggestion had merit. If he didn't know, he couldn't stop her, and the murders of their family would be examined by the greatest investigative force in the country. "Will I get any sort of training?"

"Training, along with so much more."

"And if I don't like the idea in the end?"

"You can walk away. However," he added, frowning, "you must understand I can't promise the investigation if you don't keep up your end."

She nodded. "I understand."

"Good."

In the course of their conversation, he'd managed to inch forward enough to reach out and grab her. Katria froze. His hand disappeared into his jacket pocket. Now he stood too close for her to use her rifle without falling back onto the ground if he posed a danger after all. A flash of white caught on his emerging fingers. He handed her a card.

"Be at this address in one week."

September 3rd, 832
  First Intelligence Office
  Haven City

Sean Blackbain's booted feet echoed down the long empty corridor. The dancing flames in glass lamps every few feet barely penetrated the heavy darkness of the third floor below ground level. The musk of dank walls and no sunlight thickened the air. A dense folder weighed down his left hand. He studied the name hastily scrawled across the edge.

Katerina Nachesa.

He'd never heard of the woman, who was purported to be the best shot in the world. No reputation or experience backed up the claim made by the FIO. Yet he was supposed to take her under his wing, turn her into a valuable team member. Why did he get the feeling he was being set up for something?

He glanced at the markings on the doors he walked past. Almost to the room he needed. A few feet farther, he arrived.

The door opened with ease. Three people sat inside. A lamp on the table and a low-burning fire cast the room in heavy shadow.

Ryan Voklane straddled a chair in his usual unprofessional style, his arms braced across the back. The woman's back was to him, her long black hair reflecting the meager golden light. An old man slid sheets of paper to her across the table faster than she could gather them. Shadows danced off the deep wrinkles of his face and over his gnarled hands.

Ryan glanced up and caught Sean's eye. The faint

movement caused the woman to turn around in awareness of his presence.

Impressive.

No emotion shone in her vivid blue eyes, not even curiosity as her gaze met his. In fact, as he stood and opened himself to read the emotions floating through the room, he couldn't make out any feelings from her. Like the tranquil, undisturbed surface of water, she was a void. Sean remained calm despite the phenomenon that made him want to ask a million questions. Would she still be an emotional abyss if he touched her?

He flexed the fingers on his free hand with the thought of her skin under his, and the need to encounter any emotion now. His Gen-Heir Sympathetic Empath senses, known as a Sympath, helped him pick up the bored annoyance of the old records keeper, and... *well, how interesting*, Ryan's carefully concealed anxiety. What did the liaison to the Arch Guardian of Sean's Intel team have to be nervous about?

The soft, warm light danced across the woman's ivory skin. Softly rounded cheeks, high-arched black brows, a full mouth and straight nose... he could spend hours staring at her and learning all the beautiful curves of her face. She was also young. Too young. Sean quickly looked away from her and back to Ryan.

"Can I speak with you for a moment?" he asked, motioning to the hall.

The chair feet scraped across the floor as Ryan stood. They stepped into the corridor, and Sean waited until the door closed completely before speaking.

"She's a child." He tried to control his frustration.

"She's of age, a legal adult for almost a year now. She'll be nineteen in a month."

"Voklane, what are you doing? She's not old enough, and you know it. She has zero experience and limited field training."

"She's perfect. She's completely moldable and eager to learn. Did you read her training record?"

Sean glanced down at the file he held. "I looked it over."

"And?"

"And I admit she has potential. Bring her to me in a year or two."

The normally calm demeanor Ryan portrayed shifted into hard angles and stiffened muscles. A preternatural silver glow shone across his pale blue gaze. Sean resisted the urge to step back. "We don't have a year or two. We need her now. No one else has the capabilities she has. Your team will be the greatest asset this country has, and the greatest threat to our enemies. Your Guardian team wasn't created to be second best to anyone. You'll take the woman, or I'll find someone else to lead your team."

Sean clenched his jaw. They both knew he needed to leave not only Haven City, but the whole of Sziveria. The team assignment was his long-trip ticket. He couldn't afford to mess this up. Still, there were too many concerns to ignore. Especially one. "A woman, specifically one so young, can't travel alone with three men. No story in the world we give will work."

"We already figured out how to handle that. You won't travel as a cohesive team— at least it won't appear that way. That's for the best as well. She'll travel mainly with you since you're her superior and team leader. Other times she may be with Merrick as a niece, or Dandridge as a sister. Their coloring is close enough to pull that one off."

Sean was almost afraid to ask, but he had to. "And with me?"

He gave a little smile Sean didn't trust. "Probably your ward, or whatever we need her to be." Ryan clapped him on the shoulder in a reassuring manner that made Sean want to punch him. "I'll be sure it's noted in each assignment."

"I'm sure you will."

"Oh come on, Blackbain. She's a beautiful woman. Things could be worse, really."

Sean slapped the folder against his thigh. "I'll take your word for it."

"Let's sign paperwork, shall we?" Ryan held the door open for him.

With a sinking sensation in his stomach, Sean reentered the room. The woman's gaze followed him to the table. The warm light from the fire and candle accentuated the delicate planes of her face. With her sleek midnight hair and startling blue eyes, he wasn't sure how they were supposed to travel unnoticed anywhere. He suddenly found himself thankful she wasn't standing. He didn't want to know if an equally attractive body was attached to her pretty face. Besides, he preferred women closer to his twenty-six years.

Sean flipped the chair around and took the seat closest to her, throwing the folder on the table. "Sean Blackbain. I'm your—"

"Team leader. They told me," she said softly, accepting yet another paper.

Sean barely caught the stack the old man slid to him.

He shot an impatient glance in the man's direction. "And this is?"

"Your contract."

"I already signed my contract, years ago."

"New team, new contracts and promised obligations."

"I see."

Ryan came to stand behind Sean. "You know how it is. Merrick and Dandridge signed theirs yesterday."

"Right." Sean flipped through the pages, trying to make sense of the lines of text.

"I hate to make this quick, but the MagnaRail leaving for Port Scarborough departs in thirty minutes, and you both need to be on it. Henry, the pens please, and show them where to sign."

Sean's gaze snapped up to the old man, who offered him a pen. This was happening too fast. He was supposed to have time to explain the job to this woman, go over her contract and what was to be expected of her...and what would happen if she failed. He needed to make sure she had the proper gear, the newest rifle model, and that she understood how communication worked on his team.

She'd pushed the edges of the initial few pages away, revealing the lines for her first signature, which she was poised to sign. Sean placed his hand over hers. Like threads pulling between them, the first inclination of emotion filtered through the skin-on-skin contact. Nervousness. Uncertainty. A hint of... fear. Though buried, his Gen-Heir Sympath senses drew the feelings forward. Her full lips parted, and she met his stare.

He leaned in close enough to smell the soft floral notes of her soap and see the pure, glacial-blue color of her irises. He whispered so only she could hear, "Are you *sure* you want to do this?"

Katria's heart pounded so loudly in her ears she *knew* the man sitting next to her had to be able to hear. And then he touched her, his large hand covering hers… and expected to her to form some sort of coherent thought. His amber eyes searched hers. She'd never seen eyes like his before. They seemed to glow with an inner fire.

"You have your entire life ahead of you," he said softly.

He was so close, his mouth—with a too-sensual, bow-shaped upper lip and full bottom lip—inches from her face. Katria's throat went dry. The uneven light accented the stubble covering his strong jaw and brought out the lighter streaks in the dark blond hair hanging around his face. Not a fashionable cut like Ryan's, but more rugged, his long hair falling past his shirt collar in the back. A thick piece shifted across his brow, half covering his eye, and she had the sudden urge to brush it from his forehead. She quickly looked away. This man was essentially her boss. She couldn't be thinking about anything more than the orders he would give her.

Orders.

The thought brought her back to reality.

"I'm sure I want to do this," she whispered. Then with more conviction, "I'm sure, yes."

His hand slid away from hers and she was startled by the sudden cold left behind. "Very well. Continue, please."

The old man leaned forward and with a quickness only decades in the job could provide and flipped directly to the pages they needed to sign. Katria took a deep breath with each applied signature, knowing without a doubt she signed her life away. But if it meant finding who'd destroyed her family, it'd be worth it. She'd do anything she had to now.

Ryan had assured her the case had already been handed over to operatives in both the First Intelligence and the Sziverian National Investigative Division. She just had to keep her part of the deal, and the investigation would continue. If she helped them, they'd help her.

She chanced a quick glance back at Sean. Before he'd walked in the door, attraction had been something other people experienced. No other man had ever been able to make her notice much. This man proved different. Over six-feet tall, built like he knew how to use his body as a weapon, and an appearance any sane woman wouldn't reject, had Katria noticing more than she cared to. More than she should.

He was her boss. Nothing more.

They signed the last document. A sense of finality swept over Katria. She stared at the stack of pages and swallowed against the panic. A heavy hand landed on her shoulder and she looked up.

His eyes, filled with a compassion she didn't understand, stared down at her. When had he stood? "Come on, time to go."

Closing her eyes, she filled her lungs with a soothing inward breath and then let it out. This was the last time she would allow herself to feel distress at her decision. The choice was made. Whatever happened from this day forward was the life she'd chosen. She opened her eyes and stood to follow him.

"Well, Katerina, let's see what they're having us do first."

"Katria," she corrected.

"What?"

"My name is Katria."

He cast her a quiet, searching look. "I see. How about I just call you Kat?"

A little ache formed in her heart, along with guilt she couldn't afford. "My dad calls me that… called me that, I mean. So yes, okay."

"Kat it is."

Ryan clapped in exuberance. "All right, Intel Guardian Team Blackbain, let's get this production on the rails, shall we?"

CHAPTER TWO

April 23rd, 835
  Wilhelm, Gaula

Katria carefully set the black barrel of her bolt-action combat rifle-model eighteen, referred to as a BACR-18, into its padded case laying open on her hotel bed. Next, she placed the shoulder rest and then the scope into their designated spaces. She checked her rounds for the third time, ensuring she'd have enough for the night's mission, and then locked the case.

Heavy boot falls sounded outside the room she occupied in the shared suite, and by their determined, methodical pace, she knew it was Sean and not one of the other guys. For three years she'd been a sister, niece, ward, wife, cousin, and in one instance that none of them could still figure out, an aunt. Usually she was sister or niece to Mason Dandridge, ward or cousin to Kevin Merrick, and ward or wife to Sean. Thankfully the *wife* role had happened only twice in their three years.

Katria did not need the reminder that she couldn't have him.

A soft knock sounded at her open door and she glanced up to find him standing at the threshold. "I'm almost ready."

Sean crossed his arms over his wide chest. The rolled sleeves of his dark gray cotton shirt pulled tight, revealing the defined muscles beneath. Katria fiddled with the latches on the rifle case. Anything to keep from staring.

"Mason found the house where our suspected infectious diplomat is staying," he said.

"Good, we were cutting it a little close this time."

"Can't really fault ourselves, we just received the assignment last night."

She gave a small smile. "Well, emergencies work that way, I guess."

He pushed off the doorframe and motioned with his head toward the other room. "Come on, I'm about to go over the plan."

Katria smoothed her hand down the front of her soft black dress and followed Sean to the large living area in their two-bedroom hotel suite. Kevin looked over a map laid out on a table, motioning to an area Mason tapped his finger against. Over a head taller than the other two men, with a deceptively lean build, Kevin radiated coiled strength. Katria barely came to his chest. His gold wedding ring glinted in the dying light filtering in through the dingy third story windows. He refused to take the ring off *or* even pretend he and Katria were anything but relatives. Needless to say, Kevin and Mason had become the brothers she never had.

Mason glanced up when she entered the room, his

silvery gray eyes showing warmth at the sight of her. He tossed his long black hair over his shoulder as he straightened. "Hey, Kat."

She smiled as she rounded the table and accepted his bear hug. "Nice map, as usual."

"Thanks, didn't have much time for this one."

Sean braced his knuckles on the table and leaned forward, looking over Mason's meticulous handiwork. "All right, this morning I was given orders for the team to evacuate a Cairoen diplomat suspected of having Human Rabies Syndrome. Mason did the recon we need for a successful extraction."

He nodded towards Mason, who returned the gesture in acknowledgement before Sean continued. "The Cairoen is here for a trade meeting and has been sick with cold-like symptoms for a week now. He's in denial. His country is in a panic. We're the only ones who can get him out, and hopefully home, without causing an international incident. Cairo will owe Sziveria, so we're under strict orders to get this handled."

Katria took a nervous breath. "An entire week. He has to be close to turning."

"Too close," Kevin chimed in. "That's why I'll be doing the extraction. If he goes, I can take care of him before he infects anyone else. If he's feeling as bad as the report claims, he should be holed up in his room. At least until the meeting."

"Which is tomorrow morning," Mason pointed out grimly.

"Correct. That's why we have to move this evening." Sean tapped a building across from a large house. "Kat, you'll set up here. I don't foresee any opposition. On the other hand, if we're too late, or

Kevin can't contain our diplomat friend, you'll be in a good position to make sure things stay confined." He slid his hand a couple of blocks away on the map. "Mason, you'll make sure transportation is secure, along with a direct means of getting him onto the ship without any delays. Kat and Kevin, you'll meet us at the ship. Kat, I won't have time to wait on you to get down to the street once we have him, so you and Kevin will walk the five blocks. The Cairoen's a ticking viral bomb as it is."

"Understood," Katria said.

"I'll be waiting in the carriage line with the tranquilizer ready."

"It won't work if he turns," Katria softly pointed out.

Sean sighed. "I know, but we can't forcibly detain a diplomat. If he's not infected, he won't remember much of the night with sedatives, and he can't implicate Sziveria in his abduction."

"Maybe at least cuff him after he's out. It'll slow him down if he turns on the trip," Kevin suggested.

"Okay." Sean nodded. "We can do that, but only after he's completely unconscious."

"The ship is supposed to have isolated quarters for us. First Intelligence is paying a large sum for it, and so far, no questions asked," Mason stated.

Katria leaned over the map and touched the building Mason had drawn across from their target location. "How many stories?"

"Seven, I think," Mason answered. "The bottom floor is a shop, the upper floors didn't look to be in use, so you'll have your choice." He leaned forward and tapped a narrow alley to the left of the building.

"There's an access door here, and if the lock is stubborn, a small window just down from it."

Katria nodded. "Perfect."

"We'll do a secondary communications check on location," Sean stated, glancing around. "But everyone's magnacoms worked fine when we checked yesterday?"

They all confirmed.

"Good, just make sure they're fully charged before we begin. For this mission we need to be in step-by-step contact," he ordered.

Mason and Kevin left for their own rooms to prepare. Sean rolled up the map and tossed it on the low-burning fire behind him.

Katria tsked. "I always hate that you have to burn those."

Sean looked at her. "You'd rather someone know what we're up to?"

"No, it's just Mason works for hours on those maps for us, and they're always so... real. Like you're staring at the streets from the sky. I don't know how he does it."

"Because he's a Gen-Heir," Sean replied, as if she should know as much.

Not all genetic talents were as cut and dry as hers, or even Sean's. Being touch-based, their capabilities were never in doubt. Some, like Mason, were logic-based, and required testing for proper placement in a Guardian position. Along with his high-value strategy talent, Mason's artistic abilities made him vital to the Guardian team.

She flexed her jaw in annoyance. "Yeah, I'm aware of his ability. I guess I'm still impressed by it."

He gave a small smile. "Well, we're still pretty impressed with yours."

Katria was *not* impressed with her birthed ability. So often she wished she hadn't inherited what had risen her father to rather dangerous fame. But if she dwelled on her *gift*, she'd spiral into a bad place, so she simply offered Sean a rather shallow smile. "Thanks."

Sean seemed to sense her angst. He leaned across the table and met her stare. "You aren't one of them, Kat. You aren't the people we're assigned against."

A twinge of pain constricted her heart. She had to look away from his fierce amber gaze. Over the years, they'd had variations of the same conversation. She'd always assured him she was fine, that whatever he *felt* about her was incorrect. Always put on the mantle of the emotionless assassin they'd recruited and expected. But lately, doubt grew. The kills were becoming too easy. The last handful, she hadn't even bothered to learn about her targets.

"I don't know anymore," she found herself whispering.

"I do, and I know you've read most of the files on those individuals, and you know it too."

At one time that had been true, and the information on her targets had been enough. She couldn't stop herself from wondering, though, at what point did the lack of morality at taking a life begin to take its toll? What would happen when she truly stopped caring? "Do you still care? I mean, do you care about the choices you have to make, the orders you have to give?"

He furrowed his brow. "Like tonight? No. Others, sometimes. But that's not our job to mind."

"How much longer do you think they'll keep us away?"

Annoyance flickered in his gaze; he lifted his chin towards her. "Why are you asking all this?"

She shrugged. "I don't know. Finally getting homesick, I guess."

He sighed and turned his attention back to the fire, poking the unburnt pieces of paper into the flames. "I'm not."

His answer took her by surprise. "Really? There's no one you miss?"

"I left nothing behind in Sziveria."

Katria recognized from his tone that the topic was closed. Spending three years in the man's company had given her unique insights, and this was one of them. When Sean was done talking, he was done. Since he rarely spoke about his life, she'd get nowhere with more questions.

Neither of them had given up much personal information in their three years together. Since nothing could grow beyond what was written on a piece of paper for them to accomplish, they worked hard at keeping life professional between them.

As she walked past his brooding form, watching the hint of muscles play under his shirt, she reminded herself that the less she knew about Sean Blackbain, the better.

"Coms check one – Katria reply. Over," Sean's deep voice came into Katria's ear. She gritted her teeth against the little thrill that rolled in her belly. An unwelcome reaction she wasn't allowed to have.

"This is Katria, coms check one. Over," she replied,

and then released the mic button. The bulky box attached to the belt at her hip blinked a steady green light, turning yellow at transmission. The device utilized magnetic power. She'd shaken it the entire trip to make sure it was fully charged.

The rest of the team checked in as Katria sprinted up flights of stairs, rifle case slung across her back. Small windows let in dying golden light, barely illuminating the narrow passage up. By the fifth floor her muscles protested, but she pushed through the burn in her thighs and the ache in her chest. At the seventh floor, she did a complete sweep, making sure she was alone. Only a rat scurried into a dark corner in the last room she checked.

She pressed her mic button. "Seventh floor secure, setting up in the center window. Over."

"Acknowledged."

Katria knelt and pulled the case off her back. She set the bulky container on the dusty wooden floor in front of her. Long shadows blanketed the floor. Dying light provided enough illumination for the task at hand. Years of practice allowed her to assemble the rifle in seconds. She eased a window open enough to slide her barrel into position, and then looked through the scope.

"Making entry onto the second floor," Kevin's voice said into her earpiece. *"Ballroom is full of guests, I wasn't noticed. Over."*

A faint creak sounded behind her. Katria snapped her head around and stared at the door to the room where she sat. Her free ear strained to hear another sound while she watched for telltale shadows that she wasn't alone.

Nothing.

Stupid rats.

She let out a breath and went back to looking through the scope at the party in the house below, watching for any signs that someone suspected Kevin's intrusion.

From her vantage point she had a clear view of the entire street, front of the house, gardens and walkway. A house staff meandered up a path lighting lamps as the last of the sun's rays disappeared over the horizon. The party seemed to be going smoothly enough for her to relax some. She crossed her legs and rested her rifle on the floor in front of the window. When Kevin gave the word he was on the way out, she'd reengage.

A board creaked, sharper, closer. Katria sucked in air. That was definitely not a rodent. She lifted her rifle and swung around as a groaning man, eyes rimmed red, drool flowing from his slack mouth, shuffled into the room. At one time he appeared to have been a builder, if the simple canvas pants, suspenders and long-sleeve shirt were any indication. Fingers twitching at his sides, his feet lumbered in heavy boots unevenly, his sole purpose now to find a victim. Gone was the man he'd once been.

Katria suppressed the urge to scream and reached for her mic button. The movement made the infected man notice her. He charged, fast. His weight slammed her into the rotting wall between the windows. The thin plaster caved beneath the force, splintering into the air around her. Brick and pieces of broken wood bit into her back.

All her strength focused on keeping him at arm's length. His power was no longer his own, driven by the virus's impulses. She'd seen how this story played out far too many times. It took all her mental fortitude not to panic. If his gnashing mouth bit or even touched any part of her flesh, she'd be suffering the same fate within two weeks' time.

The diseased man pressed closer until her biceps burned and trembled with the effort to keep him away. Terror ate at her and she cried out. Sweat dotted her forehead and slid between her breasts. The only choice she had was to somehow kick him far enough away to reach one of her pistols under the window, which would send her to the ground, more vulnerable than she was now.

"Something's not right," Kevin's voice said across the coms. *"He's not in his room and I'm looking at an itinerary. The meeting is happening now. Over."*

"Say again, over," Sean replied.

"We were given the wrong information. The trade meeting was scheduled for tonight, not tomorrow. Over."

"Get out of there. Kat, did you copy?" When she didn't respond, Sean said again, *"Kat, do you copy?"*

Katria gave another cry of distress as her body strained to keep the infected at bay. Teeth gnashed too close to her face. Twitching fingers attempted to grab at her with uncoordinated movements. The stench of sickness and rot made breathing difficult. Stuck, without much hope, she couldn't stop a tear from sliding down her cheek. How was she going to escape?

AVAILABLE NOW IN ALL DIGITAL FORMATS AND PRINT

My Dearest Reader,

Is there a more mysterious thing than marriage? The joining of two people, usually complete opposites in everything, forging through this great adventure called life together. As humans, we are guaranteed to make mistakes in the one relationship that will become the foundation of our family. So what does this mean for the future? How can we can look forward when we know, without question, we are destined for disappointment?

Don't focus on the negative.

Don't hold on to the mistakes.

Don't hold your spouse to an impossible standard.

What is an impossible standard? Making them responsible for your happiness. Should you be partners in joy? Absolutely! Should you be partners in achieving goals and dreams? Yes! Should they be held solely responsible for these things? No. Only *you* can find your dreams and follow your heart to them. Only *you* can find your inner joy and peace. No one else, not even the person you love, can give you this. They can be a pillar, a cornerstone, a part of what contributes, but not the only reason.

When my husband and I married (almost twenty years ago now), we were handed a pamphlet on divorce. Specifically, when I, as the wife, could divorce and expect alimony. How depressing is that? At the time, I was very young and I couldn't think beyond the next year, let alone five or even ten. There were things I'd already decided, knowing how high the divorce rate is and the reasons, we would never fight about money. We'd talk. Have conversations. My husband and I bicker, a lot, we're one of *those* couples. We don't fight, we have constructive arguments, haha. But we never go to bed angry, and when we wake up we choose to continue to love each other. Yes, choose. Love is a choice.

If you're struggling with discontentment in your marriage, consider checking out a book called *The Love Dare*. You can order it, or even find it at Hobby Lobby. I love this book because it challenges us to love our spouse again. To see them how we once did, part of a brilliant future we couldn't wait to explore. Couldn't wait to say YES to. I am still so excited about my future with my spouse. I hope, and pray, we get another twenty years. I can't wait to see where we go, what we achieve together, and as individuals (because wow, do we both have so many different things we love to do).

I hope this letter finds your marriage beautiful and blessed. Life is so much better lived with the one you love, with the one you trust to be there with you when life falls down around you. And if you're one of the ones in a happy marriage, cheers to you! Be the voice that helps strengthen the couples in your life. We all need positive reminders marriage can, and does, work.

Much Love,
Sarah Westill

SARAH WESTILL lives in Alabama with her US Army-retired husband. They have two sons – one they've successfully raised to adulthood – the other is still a work-in-progress, navigating middle school. As a full-on creative, Sarah lives to write, paint, teach, and meet amazing people while doing portrait photography. A veteran in the publishing industry working as a cover artist under the name Elaina Lee, she has been blessed to help hundreds of authors to achieve their own publishing goals for over a decade. To learn more about Sarah as she blogs her adventures, and about her Guardians, please visit her at sarahwestill.com or follow her on Instagram @authorsarahwestill

www.ingramcontent.com/pod-product-compliance
Lightning Source LLC
Chambersburg PA
CBHW010845190726
48286CB00012BA/2999

9 781955 293044